GRIFFIN
&
RENEE

WILLOW WINTERS
WALL STREET JOURNAL & USA TODAY BESTSELLING AUTHOR

From USA Today Bestselling Author Willow Winters comes a sexy, small town romance.

In this small town, everyone talks...and they all know I'm head over heels for my boss.

I didn't know I had a type until he came to town. His charming smile and rough laugh did a number on me. It's the way I found him always looking my way with his piercing gaze that really did me in.

We'd share a glance. I'd blush.
Then we'd pretend there wasn't sexual tension piled high between us.
First it was a look, then it was a touch, then it was late nights after work.

He's the owner; I serve drinks at his bar.
He comes from money; I live paycheck to paycheck.
He told me to kiss him; I did more than that.

It happened so fast, and I couldn't stop it even though I know I shouldn't have fallen for him. There's too much he doesn't know, including the very reason I could never be with him.

What we want doesn't matter, there are some secrets that never let go.

Kiss Me
In This
Small
Town

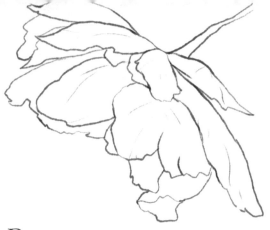

PROLOGUE

GRIFFIN

All the lights in the bar are off, floors are clean, and tables wiped down. Chair legs stick up toward the ceiling in every direction. I'm wide awake for the last few minutes of the night, but that buzz won't last long once I'm back home. Not at three in the morning. The moment my back hits that bed, everything shuts down...I think of her...and I pass out, then wake up and do it all over again. And I try to let go of what happened.

Clearing my throat, I shove it all down and go about the nightly routine.

That's something I've learned over the last few

months of owning this place. Afternoons are slow to start. The town warms up, and people trickle in for good food and even better beer. Things pick up around dinnertime and then it's in full swing into the evening. Crowds are rowdier depending on whether there's a game that night, a get-together, or a guy's night.

It stays loud and bright until just about one in the morning. Gradually, people stop shouting over the music. Renee doesn't have to talk as loud to take orders and settle tabs.

Then, finally, there's that stretch from two to three where people leave in ones and twos, some of them past ready to go and others reluctant to head home. By the time we close at three, it's usually been empty for only ten minutes. Tonight there was one holdout at two, and he went home. We cleaned up, staff left...*and now it's just me and Renee.*

It's at this moment that the tension rises. The glances happen more frequently and my pulse races with an undeniable heat. I make one last pass behind the bar, letting out a long sigh and attempting to focus on business, not her gorgeous curves. Everything's in order for tomorrow. The last glasses from the dishwasher are still warm in their rows, ready for the first orders when we open up again.

There was Renee to think of, and she's been more

distracting than anything. It feels like there's still something there. I can't be the only one feeling it. Emotions sit heavy in my stomach as she leaves and I turn off the lights, ready to leave too but not wanting to go home without saying anything to her.

The December snow falls outside in large flakes. They're coming down in lazy waves from the dark night sky. They light it up and the chill reminds me of the last few weeks.

As I zip up my jacket, I glance outside. Renee's out there, standing by her car. The streetlight above her makes the snow sparkle on her hair. She tips her head back, catching a snowflake on her face with a laugh I swear I can hear even from inside the bar. Her car puffs exhaust out into the snow. It'll be warm by the time she slides behind the wheel, which is exactly what I want for her. To be warm and safe…and with me. I want what we had back. I don't understand where it went wrong.

My boots roll quietly over the wood floor of the bar as I make my way past the shadowy booths and the waiting tables to the back door. The building keys clink on the keychain.

The first step outside feels quieter than the silence inside the bar. Snow makes everything quieter, and this late at night, there's no traffic on the street. Renee's car idles softly at the curb. It feels like we could be anywhere in the world, with nobody watching.

I like that feeling. Like we've finally got a few moments to ourselves, without having to worry about small-town gossip or other people's opinions or pretending.

I lock up the bar and test the handle. I glance back and she's still there. Maybe she does want to talk. Maybe she feels what I feel.

As my boots crunch the snow and my hands slip into my pockets to stay warm, her eyes are on me. Her red hat sets off her pink cheeks, and she gives me a slow, sad smile. It's been a long night and she's still as beautiful as the moment she stepped through the door to start her shift. More beautiful, maybe, with the snow caught in her lashes and the whole town sleeping around us.

I walk through the layer of snow in the slim parking area until I'm close enough to lean in for a kiss.

I almost make it. I can feel the heat of her breath and feel how close we are together when Renee stops me with a finger on my lips and a quiet laugh.

"It's over, isn't it? No more reason to pretend," she says, her voice clear and soft through the cold air. Is there disappointment in her tone, or am I imagining it? "Besides, you're my boss. Pretty sure you can't do that."

"Didn't stop us before," I comment and wonder if it's all in my head. If there really was nothing there for her. She only huffs a laugh and smiles. Is she teasing me?

Does she still want me? I can't tell. But I know sadness in her eyes when I see it. The question begs to be asked: *what happened?*

My heart beats hard, sending blood rushing to my face. The beat is loud in my ears now that all the noise from the evening is gone, and...this isn't how I thought this would go. Somehow, I thought...

I want to step closer to Renee, want it so bad I can taste her lips on mine, but I lean back an inch and kick at some of the rocks that came loose from the snow. I swallow down my disappointment.

I shove my hands in my pockets so I don't reach out and touch her. I don't care that we were pretending. If that's how it started...it turned into something more. Didn't it? It's killing me that she thinks that's all it was. That after everything, she still thinks it was fake.

Renee tucks her body tight to her car, her other arm over her stomach, and I think about saying it. How hard could it be to tell her the truth?

It was never pretend for me.

What we did behind closed doors...that wasn't for an audience.

It's late, and everybody in the whole damn world is asleep, and nobody has to know what we say to each other. Nobody has to know anything, but Renee should know this.

"What if—"

A pair of headlights shine on the snow, and a car rumbles along the dirt road, slow to account for the snow and the late hour. I lean back, but don't let myself take the step. What does it matter if they see? Why does anything matter except Renee?

Renee and I both watch the car go. One of its wheels dips into a groove and spins. I brace myself for it to get stuck. If that happens, I'll have to go push them out, and Renee will be gone, and it'll be too late.

Whoever's behind the wheel revs the accelerator and their wheel pops free of the groove. They keep driving until they're out of sight.

I turn back to Renee, but her eyes are still on the spot where that car disappeared into the night. It's clear the moment was broken by that car. I'm not going to get it back. She bites her lip, looking beautiful and determined, and I'm not sure I like where that look's going. Car or not, maybe I was already too late. Maybe it was never on the table for this to be real.

Renee lets out a small sigh, her breath white in the cold. It dissipates quickly, and I keep my hands pushed into my pockets.

She looks up at me, and it feels like she's a million miles away instead of half a step across a snow-covered dirt parking area.

"All the what ifs don't add up when it comes to us, Griffin."

There's a beat where I think she might take it back, but her face doesn't fall and her eyes don't soften and she doesn't. She opens the driver's side door of her car and climbs in.

I wrap my hand around the top of the doorframe as she puts on her seatbelt. It clicks into place, and I want to reach down and undo it. I could take her hand and pull her out of the car and kiss her. Remind her of what it feels like. My fingers tighten on the doorframe, but I can't be the guy who chases her if she doesn't want to be chased.

I have to force myself to loosen my grip.

"Get home safe, Renee."

"You, too." Her hands are on the wheel. She looks up at me, and there's something in her eyes that makes my stomach sink. It makes me sure that someday, she's going to leave this town, and I'm never going to see her again.

I open my mouth to say something. I could tell her not to drive away. I could admit to the feeling that's taking up my whole chest. I could make her promise not to leave town.

Based on what? Something she thinks is *pretend?*

There's a hint of indecision in her eyes, but then she takes a breath, and I don't want her to tell me to shut the door. I don't want to make her *ask* me to back away.

"Good night," I tell her, and shut the door for her.

Renee turns away and reaches for something on the dash. Her headlights turn on, and they splash against the back door of the bar. It looks empty in the light, almost abandoned, and that's not how it felt a few minutes ago. It felt cozy, all tucked in for the night, but that was only because she was waiting out here for me.

I turn my back on Renee and stride over to my own car. She looks out her window and lifts her hand to wave to me.

I wave back.

Then she backs out of her spot, her tires cutting new tracks in the snow, and pulls carefully out onto the road. Renee pauses to make sure there's no traffic, even though there hasn't been another car since the one that drove by, then starts down the road.

I wasn't going to stand here and watch her leave, but that's what I end up doing. Her tail lights flash red a couple of times as she makes her way down the road. I can see her silhouette in the front seat when the moonlight hits her just right. I don't have enough time to watch her before she turns on her blinker, stops, waits...

And goes.

And then she's gone, and the road's dark. Bar's dark. Sky's dark, covered in winter clouds.

I swallow hard, then unlock my car and dig my ice

scraper out from the back seat. There's no ice tonight, just a thin layer of snow. I brush it all off the car and watch it fall away, disappearing as it goes. Then I drop into the driver's seat. The leather's cold and feels pretty damn unwelcoming after the warmth of the bar and the warmth of Renee. I pull the door shut behind me, shutting out the wind, and start the car.

Maybe I should have run after her.

I don't know what to do when she won't tell me what happened. She plays it off with shy smiles and sweet laughs. But something happened.

"It wasn't pretend for me," I whisper. It's too late for Renee to hear me, but I have to get the words out anyway. I flick on the headlights, and they light up a piece of the empty road, some dark trees, and the rest of the night without her. "I think I love you, Renee."

I let my head fall back against the headrest.

Nobody heard me say it, but that doesn't seem to matter.

"Fuck," I admit in the silence, not knowing how to tell this woman she is breaking my heart, and I think it's because hers was broken too badly long ago. "I know I love you, and it's not the same for you." I wish she'd let me fix it. If only I knew what happened, I'd make it right. I fell in love with her...and I'd have to be blind not to see that she fell in love with me, too.

Chapter 1

Griffin

Three Weeks Prior

December 1st

The afternoon light hits differently. It's softer yet brighter and brings a warm glow to the dark wood in the bar. I glance at the clock and note it's at the tail end of the lunch rush, and everything is just how it should be. Plenty of free stools at the bar, and it's not too crowded. There's room for anybody who walked in right now, and we haven't reached the part of the evening where couples come in on dates or the games start drawing a crowd.

I didn't always like the slow part of the day. In college,

I liked it best when the bar was bursting at the seams with the music too loud and everybody yelling over it. Back then it felt like anything could happen if you ordered just the right drink and talked to just the right girl. Nothing was too serious, and every day was a fresh start. Life could have taken me anywhere. Every time Brody and I went down Main Street bar hopping and talking up big dreams of owning our own bar one day, I thought I wanted something new. Another girl would lean up next to the bar, and my imagination would run away with me.

It's funny how dreams change.

Or...how they get more specific. Brody found what he was looking for and damn did he get something he never could have imagined. There are a million places in the world you can buy a bar or build one, and there're a million ways it can look, but we settled on this one, close to my hometown, but far enough away to do it however we wanted.

It was just a conversation at first, and then it was money, and then it was sweating and sawing and installing fixtures and reading up on building codes and city ordinances until my eyes burned from lack of sleep and my shoulders were heavy with stress. We had to file for permits and get our licenses in order and... every fucking little thing you don't know you need until someone tells you that you do.

Now it's real.

I'm proud and grateful....and now I can't deny along the way I realized what I was missing.

Renee leans over a table in the corner and puts down the bill in its folder like she's giving the patrons a gift, and that's how they take it. The two men in blue jeans and polo shirts give her big smiles and look her in the eye. Everybody brightens up a little looking at Renee. She's got an air about her that just makes you smile.

She walks off, her hips swaying, and I get the impression she doesn't know just how gorgeous she is. Her auburn hair drapes down her back from the low ponytail and sways with her walk. It takes every ounce of effort for my eyes not to fall to her hips and then to the gorgeous curves of her ass in those tight blue jeans. Fuck, I suppress a groan just in time for her to look back at me, and I give her a tight-lipped smile. I swear her wicked hazel eyes flash a knowing look. Heat rises up my chest but just as quickly as she looked back, she turns away and I'm left with a racing heart and a feeling no woman has ever made me feel.

And I'm thinking...

How do I make her fall for me?

Because I don't mind looking at her like she's beautiful and kind and I'm lucky just to get to talk to her.

But I want her to look at me like she's finally found the man she wants to spend the rest of her life with. I want her to look at me like the world's bright just because I'm in it.

The bar *is* special—it's my bar, after all—but Renee makes it shine. Look at her. It's just an ordinary day, and somehow the light in her hair is like nothing I've seen before, and when she smiles, it makes my heart skip a beat. The music and the chatter fade to nothing when I look at her.

A nudge at my elbow takes me out of my thoughts.

"You should take a picture, you know?"

I look over at Patty, my fellow bartender on this shift. She raises her eyebrows at me. Damn. She caught me staring, and Patty knows what she's talking about. She's older, married, and damn good at her job. I almost can't picture Iron Brewery without her, but that means she notices everything that goes on in the place...including who I'm looking at. Nothing gets past Patty.

My face gets hot and my heart's already beating fast from watching Renee, but I ignore all that and give her a shocked look. "I wasn't—"

"Please, Griffin, you were enjoying the view." Patty tips her head back and laughs. I don't think it was that obvious, but how loud she's laughing says otherwise. It tapers off after a second and she scans the bar. "Need another, Sam?"

Sam, a patron at the far end of the bar, shakes his head. Patty gives him a thumbs-up. From the looks of his glass, it won't be long until he'll be flagging her down, but Patty never rushes anybody on their drinks. I think it's half the reason she's so good. Even when somebody frankly needs a fire under their ass, Patty never seems like she's pushing.

Renee walks away from the table and meets up with Mary Sue, one of the other waitresses. She's a sweet redhead, one of those girls everybody calls fresh-faced, and she's got bright green eyes.

I catch myself staring this time and once again trying to pretend that I'm not doing it.

It doesn't help at all because Renee's on the move. She goes to the other side of the bar and wipes down the counter. A song with a good beat plays just loud enough to make the bar lively, and Renee swings her hips to the beat. That girl must know exactly what she looks like, dancing like that. She's gorgeous, she's tempting, and sooner or later I'll figure out a way to make her fall for me. I'll figure out how to be the kind of man Renee would fall for.

I don't want to get caught staring a third time, so I look out over the bar. It's spacious but still cozy thanks to the lighting. Iron Brewery is a classic neighborhood bar with sturdy stools pulled up to the bar, booths along one side, and tables in the middle. We've got a window in front looking out on the main street and a smaller window in back with a view of a less-prestigious road.

It's brand new with a modern feel and everything Brody and I dreamed of. Plus, anybody who spends time in bars like this knows that a neighborhood bar picks up pieces of the neighborhood and all the people who live there. In a town the size of this one, that's pretty much the whole town. Everyone knows everyone and that reminds me of home. I mean this place is my new home...and not too far away from where I grew up. But there's something about owning this bar that just adds a feeling of belonging to this town.

I'm proud of the place. Brody and I put a fuckton of hours into it when we first bought the place. I practically slept with my to-do list. The only thing that ever slowed me down was stepping on a nail when I was wearing flip-flops, which cost me a trip to the ER for a tetanus shot. After that, I bought the sturdiest work boots they sold at the hardware store.

It probably should have been impossible to get the place up and running in the amount of time we did, but it was worth it.

"Hey, Patty?" Sam lifts his glass. Patty nods back to him, and he thanks her.

Turning my head in that direction is a dangerous game because Renee's still dancing and looking at the way her body moves affects my entire blood supply.

My phone buzzes in my back pocket. Perfect timing. I need a distraction if I'm not going to get a raging hard-on at work.

I take my phone out and lean back against the counter.

Brody: *Hey, I can't come in*

Brody: *She's still sick with the flu and I've been staying up all night, I'm exhausted*

I feel him on that. I don't have any kids myself, but keeping the bar running smoothly means a lot of late nights. Sometimes, when I'm up 'til close, I can't get to sleep afterward, and when the sun rises, that's it.

Doesn't mean you don't feel guilty. I know Brody does. He goes all in on everything he does, and he thinks he should be superhuman. I can tell he feels bad even if he doesn't say another word.

But sometimes, one person has to carry more of the load. By this point, I'm more than prepared. We've had the bar open for long enough that I can run it myself with the waitresses, cooks, and bartenders. Brody can get a couple hours of sleep, if fate will let him.

Griffin: *No worries, everything is under control*

Griffin: *Seriously, I got it*

I glance over, and Renee isn't dancing anymore.

She's talking to Patty with their heads leaned together. Nobody catches me looking, but the back of my neck heats up. My phone buzzes before I can think too much.

Brody: *Thanks man, I owe you*

Griffin: *No you don't*

I put my phone back into my pocket just as Renee laughs at something Patty said. The back of my neck gets hotter, and the heat goes all over my chest.

Patty wouldn't do me like that I don't think. But that laugh...my God it does something to me. My heart races and suddenly Renee's all I can think about. I should be ashamed of where my mind goes.

They're not thoughts I should be having at work or about my employee, but I can't stop them for anything.

Just when I think I'm going to have to excuse myself to the bathroom and splash cold water onto my face, the door to the bar opens.

"Griffin!"

The sound of my name cuts off my thoughts. I take a deep breath of the fresh air that swoops in before the door shuts and turn to find my mother. She has a huge grin on her face and waves at me across the bar, then looks around like it's a five-star restaurant and I've just won a prize for the best bar in the world.

"Hey, Mom," I call. "You stopped by just in time."

CHAPTER 2

RENEE

In the months I've worked at the bar, nothing this exciting has ever happened before.

Unless you count my boss coming to work every day, which is exciting for all the wrong reasons.

Whenever Griffin comes through the door, my body lights up from the tip-top all the way down to my tiptoes. Some parts lighting up hotter than others. I've had dreams about him smiling at me at the beginning of a shift and the soft way he says my name. I've probably thought about my boss for at least twelve hours a day since I started working here.

The truth is, I don't know how to stop having a crush on Griffin. Even if I moved to another town, I'd still think about him and how charming his smile is. I can't help but to smile myself even when I'm just thinking about that look he gives me.

It might be ridiculous for me to crush so hard on a man I know I shouldn't lust over...I won't take the blame for how handsome he is, though. I didn't have anything to do with that. I just have to live with it every single time I come in to work a shift.

This shift however, I was not expecting his mother to walk in. I've never met his family, and I have no right to feel as anxious as I do.

It's nothing to be nervous about, but here I am with clammy hands and a racing heart. I watch as Griffin walks over to his mom with extended arms and gives her a hug and a kiss on the cheek. I have the urge to run to the nearest mirror and make sure my hair is smoothed back, and then I get ahold of myself and check on my tables instead.

Nerves flutter in my chest, but I shake them off. It's just Griffin's mom, and Griffin is just my boss. It's not like we can ever be together or anything like that.

I try not to listen as they talk behind me. Swallowing down the ridiculous emotions, I look out the front window to steady myself. A few snowflakes come down from a mostly blue sky. It won't be light for much longer, and I don't mind it. The bar seems cozier in the evenings. The farther we get into the winter, the more people seem to appreciate being here.

That's enough to get my head on straight and get back to work. I took this job because I need the money. And that's what this is. A job.

Both of my tables need their drinks refreshed, so I zip around with two Diet Cokes and a beer. The guy at table two wants more fried pickles. The lady he's with debates dessert, so I tell her the brownie is my favorite, because it really is. The trips back and forth to the kitchen window take my mind off Griffin for a few seconds at a time. I can't help looking at him every time I turn around, though.

He shows his mom around the bar and her eyes light up with pride. He's taller than she is, and she's wide-eyed and in awe, giving everything a once-over like Griffin made it by hand. It's sweet and genuine. He must be so happy to make her proud.

I know he installed most of the booths himself, and he and Brody both worked on refinishing the floor and sanding down the bar, which was probably a huge time-sink. So it makes sense that she'd understand what a huge accomplishment this place is. Heck, even I'm in awe of what Griffin can do.

A blush flares in my cheeks as my thoughts wander and I have to force myself to look away and get back to work.

Griffin takes her around by the booths, pointing down the row and then back up at the front window. He keeps his voice low enough that I can't hear what he's saying, but that's good, because I don't want to eavesdrop on his conversation with his mother.

But then he laughs and gestures out the window. "Yeah, we had everybody in here. Too many people for the fire code, and I had to get a special license to sell drinks on the sidewalk and put up a barrier."

His mother's smile widens, and I remember that night and smile to myself about it. Griffin seemed surprised that everybody wanted to watch the game and celebrate at Iron Brewery, but it didn't surprise me. It's the kind of place that's comfortable, and people know it well. Hopefully next time he won't have to put up cones on the sidewalk.

Or maybe, if the weather's nice, he could extend the space out back.

The tables in the middle seem to lead straight to Griffin and his mom, and they're not all full, so I almost can't help looking.

Griffin's mom laughs at his story and it's then I realize I don't know her name. It's so obvious that she loves him. I know from working together that he grew up in a small town that's a couple hours down the highway. I think most people end up back where they started, so it's a really lucky break that Griffin and Brody ended up here.

Shoot. I find myself staring again. I quickly look away and glance at anything and everything else.

I put the crush out of my mind as much as I can. Some days, I can go an hour without thinking *I have a crush on my boss* and other days, like this one, I can't make it fifteen minutes.

Griffin turns toward the bar, and I get on the move again and wipe down some of the free tables just to make sure they're up to snuff. Patty comes out from behind the bar, and Griffin introduces his mom to her. She shakes Patty's hand and has another wide smile, as if to say, *look what my son did, isn't it incredible?* It's so sweet that I get flutters again and wipe down a few more tables to burn off the energy.

One more drink refill—another Diet Coke—and I go to ring up the first of the tables to finish. They hand over a credit card right away, so I cash them out and wish them a pleasant afternoon.

On the way back to the bar, I catch Griffin gesturing at me out of the corner of my eye and my heart starts pounding. I put on my best meeting-Griffin's-mom smile and head over to them. Patty's back behind the bar pouring some beers, so it's just me, and I'm more nervous than I was at my first interview.

"Hi," I say, even though Griffin's been here for almost my whole shift.

Griffin opens his mouth.

"You must be Renee!" His mom says and holds out her hand.

"I am." I shake hands with her, my face hot. I don't know what to do other than smile, because I'm holding back the question of how she knew that.

I get my answer when I peek over at Griffin, and he's blushing.

My temperature rises again, all through my body. It's a good thing opening the door let in some fresh air, because I might be glowing with sweat by now, and nobody needs that.

It's more complicated than me having a crush on Griffin. He has a crush on me, too, or at least I've always thought that he did. The blushing in front of his mom is proof. I'm not the only one dealing with feelings every shift, no matter how hard I try not to let it affect my work.

I've caught Griffin looking at me more than once, which makes me feel those butterflies in the pit of my stomach. I try not to feel his eyes on me when I'm working. It's never in a way I don't want, and always makes this push and pull seem almost romantic and magical.

Neither of us has made a move, which is the right

thing to do given our circumstances and everything going on in my personal life.

Besides being the right thing, it's just something I'm grateful for. Some days I'm so grateful for it that I get choked up.

The truth is that I need this job more than I've needed almost any job in my lifetime. After everything that happened, I'm behind on my bills, and that means working twice as hard to get caught up and in a stable place again. My goal this year is to trust only myself and get back on my own two feet. That's my *only* goal. It's not to fall in love with my boss or act on my crush and get myself into another situation where I'm behind.

I can't afford to have things at this job go sour.

"How do you like it at Iron Brewery, Renee?" Griffin's mom asks with the same proud expression.

"Oh, I love it here." I keep my eyes away from Griffin when I say it. "It's nice to work in a place that means something to people."

"I've always said that the people make the place." Griffin's mom puts her hand on Griffin's arm, and he gets redder. I struggle to keep my smile from widening.

"Mom," he says. "It's not just me. Everyone who works here is a part of it."

"I can see that," Griffin's mom says knowingly, and I wonder just how much he's talked about me—about all of us—to his mom. From the way she seemed thrilled to meet Patty, it's probably a lot.

It's easy to see where Griffin's excitement and kindness come from. A good man from a good family.

"So, what's on tap for the afternoon?" Patty bustles out from behind the bar and joins us with a knowing look on her face. Her eyes sparkle like she's just as excited about Griffin's mom visiting as he is. It makes sense, because she's just as proud of Iron Brewery as Griffin is and puts more heart into the bar than almost anybody else. If I wasn't around when Brody and Griffin put the place together, I'd think she was around here even longer. "Are you taking your mom for the full tour of the town? You really should, you know. We've got a great place here."

"We do," I agree, and maybe that's why Griffin's eyes settle on me. They drop down to my lips and come back up to my eyes. This one time, I let myself look back at him. He's just so attractive that it's almost impossible to look away, and it would be weird if I looked down at my shoes.

A smile crosses Griffin's face. "Yeah, we do."

I didn't think I could blush any harder, but I'm pretty sure it's happening. With Patty and Griffin's mom standing here with us, I just have to look at his handsome face and keep my smile still, because if I say another word, they'll both know I'm into him, and then I'll never live it down.

So I smile and smile, falling deeper into his eyes every second.

Griffin shakes himself, like he was falling too, and puts his hand on the back of his neck to rub at the skin there. "But now's not the right time for a town tour."

Patty raises her eyebrows, but she's still smiling a little, which makes me think she knows more than she's letting on. "It isn't? The weather isn't bad, and there's still enough daylight to see everything."

"Not yet." Griffin drops his hand. He still hasn't stopped looking at me. "I thought we'd stay here for a while and have lunch."

CHAPTER 3

GRIFFIN

My mom settles back into her seat across from me in my favorite booth. There's a good view of the bar from this corner seat, plus I can watch the front doors.

My mom's eyes flick over everything from the napkin holder and the framed photo of the main street on the Fourth of July and even the light fixture above us like she hasn't seen all the videos I've sent her.

"So," she says. "Tell me about this town. It's small... even smaller than our hometown."

"I'd say it's just the right size." The bar is just the right size, too. Enough space to have a good crowd for the big games, not so much that it feels like a corporate chain restaurant. We have a row of booths along one side and tables in the middle—not too many, not too few. A decent number of seats at the bar. In the summer, we can seat people on the side patio, where we've got wrought iron tables with blue-and-white umbrellas. Like most places in town, we're busier in the summer, a little slower in the winter, and it all works out fine.

This place was a hardware store before it was Iron Brewery, so Brody and I didn't go into it wanting to change everything. It's got old bones that stood the test of time but new tables, booths, chairs, and flooring. We refinished the bar and made sure it was set to go for another twenty years. Most of the bar stools are original to the place, but we had a few new ones made to match the ones that were on the way out.

"How's it just the right size?" she questions with a tilted smirk that makes me think she knows something.

"I don't know, it just..." I put my hands up, but there are really too many things to list. "It's a nice place to live. There's everything I need right here. You should see the sailboats, Mom. There's something going on every weekend during the winter. If you need something, you can talk to your next-door neighbor, and that's true for the businesses, too. That is what I mean by just the right size."

"Is everyone from here? Renee?" she asks, and I can see right where this line of questioning is headed.

Luckily, I'm saved by the bell.

"It's the kind of small town where everyone knows everyone, and yup, they all grew up here," Brody says, joining us at the table. He slides into the seat next to my mom, and she kisses his cheek, brightening up even more.

He looks like he could use a shave and like he threw on whatever shirt was closest just to get out of the house, but thank fuck Brody's here. My mother has started calling him her adopted son, and honestly I could use the distraction. "How was your trip over?" he asks her.

"Just as uneventful as I could've hoped for," she answers. "I almost listened to a whole audiobook."

"Good. I was worried about the roads," Brody says. "It looked like it might storm. I don't want you driving in that."

"Oh, stop it. It almost never snows around here." My mom waves him off, blushing. "How is Magnolia?"

"She's..." Brody takes a deep breath and smiles before he lets it out. "Pregnant."

She slaps him lightly on the arm but laughs playfully, and Brody laughs with her. He talks to my mom almost as much as I do, mostly because my mother is a busybody and I stopped answering her questions about Brody. So she went right to the source. I'm glad he has my mom. He's been through a lot and his family is farther away.

"Is she liking pregnancy?" My mother pushes and I can't help but notice how she leans in. The back of my neck feels hot knowing how much my mother wants grandbabies. It's all she ever talks about now.

"She's doing okay," he goes on. "Due in a month, though, so she's tired and uncomfortable and ready for the baby to come. She's been great most of the time, no problems, so I hope that won't change."

Brody goes on about Mags and how great she is and how beautiful she is when she's pregnant. I lean back, happy for my friend as his eyes light up every time he says her name. It takes me back to when the two of us were friends in high school. Back then, we had no idea what we'd end up doing with our lives. My main plan was to go to college, but it felt like the world was wide open. I could have landed anywhere from here to California. I spent a lot of time thinking about starting a new life in a new town that nobody had heard of.

Then Brody would flick a paper football at me, and I'd stop thinking about all that stuff. He always had a smile on his face back then. He was the kind of guy who could do anything with his life, and for a while after high school, he did.

Now that I'm looking back on it, it seems almost like a

miracle that we've ended up doing this. We had all those possibilities, and we chose to open a bar together. Maybe I didn't know it was my dream to do this back then, but the more we talked about it, the more it became a goal I had to achieve.

And now I'm actually living out my dream, owning a bar with my best friend.

But all I keep thinking about now is...what's next? I have my dream life, and I would sound like an asshole if I complained. How many people get to go into business with their best friend and have it succeed? How many people get to own a place like Iron Brewery, where you're guaranteed to see even more of your friends almost every day and make new ones just as often?

Not that many.

The one thing that's different is that Brody has Mags now. That's not a bad thing. That's a great thing. They deserve to have each other and deserve to be happy.

But watching him talk about her reminds me of the emptiness I feel every time I see them together and every time Brody tells a story about her. I never thought I'd feel that because my best friend found the love of his life before I did.

Mary Sue stops by the table to take our orders. "Hi, Mrs. Matthews! It's so nice of you to stop by and spend some time here."

My mom preens, looking happy to be a small-town celebrity. We place our orders, starting with Mom, who orders a crispy chicken sandwich, and ending with Brody's and my orders of burger and wings,

Mary Sue glances from me to my mom. "You're from just up north, right?"

Mom nods at her. "Yes, ma'am. A little place called Orangeburg."

"Not as little as here, I think," Mary Sue says, and we all laugh.

"A little bigger." My mom holds out her thumb and forefinger about an inch apart.

"Let me get these orders in for you." Mary Sue taps her pen against the pad she's scribbled on and makes her way to the kitchen.

My mom asks a few more questions about Mags, and then there's a short lull in the conversation while we sip our drinks. Absently I scrunch up the straw paper into a little ball and glance back to where Renee just was. She's not there anymore though...probably in the back by the kitchen.

"Are you seeing anybody, Griffin?" Mom asks casually, just when I'm getting ready to ask her about the family holiday plans this year.

Brody chuckles, and I wave off my mom, ignoring the way my face heats up again. I have to stop blushing in front of her, or she'll have questions from here to next New Year's. I don't mind that she asks about my life. I love that I can tell her almost everything. But *these* kinds of questions—

"What?" My mom says, her eyebrows raised and an innocent expression on her face. "Isn't that what's next?"

Brody nods, taking her side, and I shoot him a look. He's been my best friend for almost half my life. He should know better than to side with my mom. Although it does earn him a hell of a lot of brownie points.

My mom raises both hands in front of her. "All I meant was that I hope you can find a date to bring to Christmas dinner."

"She has a point," Brody says, leaning back in the booth, and I make a conscious effort to not flick the ball of paper at him.

"Even our old neighbors, the Bennets, have settled down," she points out. "Don't you think—"

Now *that* makes me feel like I'm in high school again. My mom tried to hide it, but she was more excited than anybody about homecoming and prom. She casually lurked around the living room in the evenings, not really watching TV, just waiting to see if I'd spill who I was going to ask. She'd always say, *what? I just want you to have the best time.*

"Come on, Mom. When I get a girlfriend, I'll let you

know. Right now there're no secrets to spill."

I just wish she wouldn't push so hard—especially when the girl I have eyes for is my best friend's wife's best friend and my employee. If I went for Renee and it didn't work out, it would cause so many issues between all four of us. One wrong move could literally make my entire life harder, at home and at work, and I'm not even the one I'm most worried about. I don't want to screw anything up for Renee or make her feel awkward at work or make her feel like she can't talk about it to her best friend.

"Mags is thinking about taking a road trip once the baby's a little older," Brody says. "A low-key getaway."

"I love road trips." My mom turns her attention back to Brody, which is the second time he's saved my ass during this conversation. "Have you thought about going out west? I have a book of the best national parks to stop at. It's a little outdated, but I can't imagine the parks have changed much."

"Isn't the point of the parks to stay the same?"

"I guess so," my mom says, laughing. "I visited Yellowstone—oh, what was it, fifteen years ago now? Twenty? You think a picture does it justice, but when you see it with your own eyes, it's something else."

You know who's something else? Renee. I wouldn't mind a trip to Yellowstone, or any of the national parks, but I can't think of anything more stunning than her face.

And then my mind is off and running, thinking about Renee in the passenger seat of my car, her hair blowing around her face and big sunglasses on, the two of us speeding down the highway for a *real* low-key getaway. No babies, no work responsibilities, just the two of us escaping for a while.

None of it makes that much sense because Brody's the one who's into backpacking and camping and spending time in the wilderness, but I could be into backpacking if Renee was.

Is she into backpacking?

There's never been a reason to talk about what vacation we'd take if we had a tank full of gas, a couple weeks off work, and no business to take care of, because I've never asked her about her vacation plans. Renee's focused on working when she's at work, as she should be, and I'm focused on not getting caught staring at her as much as I can. That's probably the type of flirty conversation I shouldn't even imagine having with her.

I let out a groan and rub my hands over my face.

"You all right?" Brody asks, looking concerned.

"Yeah." I drop my hands to the table. "Just remembered a couple, uh, bills I have to pay. And I have to buy stamps."

My mom and Brody both look at me like I've said

something they can't understand. Most bills you can pay online now, and you don't need stamps, so that's probably it. I'll double down on it if I have to, because we are not going to discuss my crush on Renee or the fantasy road trip I just spent several minutes picturing.

"Griffin—" my mom starts.

"Who's hungry?" Mary Sue appears at the side of the table with a big tray balanced on her palm.

"I am," I tell her, and lean back in my seat to make room for the food. My mom exclaims over everything, and Brody compliments her choice of order. I stay quiet to keep myself out of trouble.

Because the most honest thing I could say is that the food looks great, it always does, but what I'm really hungry for is Renee...and I'm pretty sure everyone knows it. Including her.

CHAPTER 4

RENEE

"Do you think you'll have a baby sprinkle, then?" I turn the corner at the largest baby store for miles around, which happens to be in the next town over, and glance at my best friend Mags. She's walking slow at my side, and I pace myself so she doesn't feel rushed. She's round, and every few minutes her eyes close like she's struggling to stay on her feet. The baby has dropped, and I don't think Mags is going to make it to the new year.

Mags is due in the next month, which is pretty much any day in terms of being pregnant. She takes every step like she's really thinking about it and rests both hands on her belly, alternating every few steps with putting them on her hips. She looks cute as a button in her maternity clothes. She's always cute, but the top she has on really suits her.

Her wedding dress suited her, too. She got married in the autumn when she was six months pregnant. It seems like the time since then has flown by. I can't imagine what it feels like for her. In the back of my mind, as we walk through the aisles I know this time is going to be different for her.

"No baby shower," she says and then takes a deep inhale. "We don't need anything and besides, this one is the second." We pass the wall of strollers as my brow arches. They're all shoulder-height off the ground, and I guess you're supposed to lift them down if you want to test them out. I don't trust myself to lift one of those over both our heads. Whose idea was it to put them up so high?

"If you don't want a shower, that's fine, but we can have a sprinkle."

Mags shakes her head, swishing her blonde hair, and sighs as she reaches up to touch one of the tires on the nearest stroller. It's a sturdy piece of rubber. A baby riding in this thing wouldn't feel even the slightest bump.

Mags drops her hand back to her belly and nervously

chews at her bottom lip. "I don't know, Renee. I don't want the attention, you know?"

My heart hurts for her, because I know how much it matters to have these kinds of moments in your life celebrated. This is a moment to celebrate even if it's not Mags' first baby. Besides, last time was years ago and so, so different.

Maybe it's selfish of me, but I want a chance to show Mags how excited I am for this little one. How so many people in her life are excited and happy for her. Brody missed out last time, I almost say but bite my tongue. The past is the past for a reason.

"What about a sip and see?" I offer. We make our way a bit farther down the aisle and stop at a bassinet that's set up for display. "When the baby is here...just a little sip and see?" My voice turns a higher pitch filled with a touch of hope and a little optimism.

Mags tilts her head to the side and runs her hand along the edge of the bassinet. "This is cute," she says, almost to herself. Then, to me, she asks, "No gifts?"

My expression straightens with a look that makes her crack a smile. "Who would come to a sip and see and not bring gifts?"

Mags shakes her head again, her smile slipping, and we move on to a shelf full of the best bottles in the world according to the advertising on the display.

"Just like a real nipple," Mags reads. "Wow. That's kind of in your face."

"Well, I guess nipples are in your face when you're a baby."

She snorts, then laughs louder. I join in because it is a pretty out-there display. "Stop," she says, and bumps me with her elbow. "Stop, I'm going to pee my pants."

"Sorry!" I put on my most serious face and go as silent as I can.

Mags breathes in deep, then lets it out slow. "Where *is* the bathroom in this place, anyway?"

"Behind us." I point. "Do you think you can make it, or should I pick you up and carry you?"

She rolls her eyes at me, and we detour to the bathroom, which luckily is only a few steps away. Mags takes a minute to catch her breath afterward.

"Even pulling up my pants is a workout," she says, grumbling in a lighthearted way. Her cheeks are pink just from our slow walk, and she glances down at her belly and gives it a smile.

"So, for the sip and see..." I continue as we leave the bathroom.

Mags makes a face. She's resistant to the idea, and I can tell. It's probably because of her last pregnancy and the way the town spread rumors. That's the downside of living in a small town. Everyone knows your business, and sometimes they don't take news the way you hope they will. And we all know people who can blow just about anything out of proportion in the wrong direction.

"Come on, Mags." I use my gentlest tone with her, because she's my friend and she deserves gentleness... and also because she deserves everything else that comes along with welcoming a new baby. "When the little one is here, everyone is going to want to see him or her, and it'll be so nice if you could get pampered along with the baby."

"Ugh. I don't know." We turn down the next aisle, which is full of baby clothes in every color of the rainbow. Tiny overalls and even tinier onesies. Socks that fit in the palm of my hand. Sleep suits that could fit a teddy bear. My heart does a slow flip-flop thinking of holding Mags' baby in one of these outfits. Mags holds up a pair of baby shoes, her eyes shining. "Babies can't walk, so it's not even practical to buy shoes, but this stuff makes me teary-eyed."

"They're *so* cute. Anything in miniature is cute."

"I don't need them. The baby probably won't need them either. I want to buy everything in this aisle so much."

I wait a minute. "What if you let the rest of us buy you *some* of it? It doesn't have to be a big deal. Just a calm, casual sip and see while you relax and show off your little baby. We'll tell you how beautiful they are in quiet voices so they don't wake up from their nap."

Mags looks at the ceiling, then back down at those shoes.

"Just think about it?" I offer. "I'd be thrilled to plan it for you. You wouldn't have to do a thing, and I'd really love to do it."

"I—"

"Don't decide now. Seriously, just think about it, okay? And I think Bridget would have so much fun with it."

Mags looks at me, a hesitant smile on her face. She's beautiful. When they talk about pregnant women glowing, this is what they mean. She looks almost radiant, and it's so different from the last time. Her happiness is right on the surface.

Mags got her happily ever after, and I've never been happier for anyone. It almost makes me feel like I'm glowing, too. Compared to her last pregnancy this is night and day, and nobody deserves this day more than Mags.

"Butter," she says.

"What?" I laugh.

"Belly butter," she says tapping a single finger on her swollen belly. "I need some. The biggest tub they have for the biggest belly I've ever had."

"Your perfect belly," I tell her, and we make our way around to the section for moms-to-be before heading out with only the tub of butter. The cashier compliments her, too.

Then we head out to the car. A gust of December wind flies right into our faces on the way, and I grab for Mags' arm to make sure she's steady.

"I'm fine!" she shouts, laughing. "I've done this before, remember?"

"Besides," she says as she opens the car door, "I don't think a gust could blow me over." I have to laugh at her joke.

In the car I get behind the wheel and turn the heat up full blast. Somehow it feels like the car's been sitting out here for days instead of forty minutes. The heat works well, though, so we won't be cold for long.

There's a peaceful quietness as we drive off.

I check both ways at the exit of the parking lot and make the first turn toward the highway. We cruise along listening to the music as we head back toward town.

"So," I say, after a mile or two. "Did you decide on names yet?"

"I've thought of about a hundred, but every morning I wake up and I've changed my mind."

"Does Brody have any favorites?"

Mags grins, her cheeks flushing. "He goes along with whatever my idea of the day is. If he has a special favorite he hasn't told me what it is yet."

"He's such a good dad."

"Yeah," Mags says, agreeing, smiling wider. "Even if he doesn't have the first clue how to change a diaper."

Mags tells me cute stories about Brody the rest of the way to her place. She teases, but it's easy to see how much she loves him. When we get there, I drive up as close to the front porch as I can and hand her the bag with the belly butter.

"I love you!" I shout through the windshield as she makes her way up the stairs, holding the railing for balance. Mags blows me a kiss. I wait until she's inside, then drive to my place.

For the longest time it was just us. Time has changed that and it's harder for me to share with her what's happening in my life when hers is finally going right. I know she'd want me to lean on her, but I just can't. One of us deserves happiness.

It's not long before I'm at my apartment, thoughts and memories running through my head. My place is small and cozy and lived in, with wood floors and a large paned window in the living room. This is my little escape from the world and as soon as I'm through the front door I let out a heavy breath, toss my keys on the skinny foyer table, and flick on the light.

Then I hang up my coat and my purse and put my tips from last night into a five-gallon jug I keep by the door. It's filling up little by little, and when it's full... well it feels like if only I can do that, I can take care of other things.

As I pull my hair to the side, absently braiding it to keep the strands out of my face before sagging into my safe area, my phone buzzes.

It's a text from my mom.

My blood goes cold as I read it: *I'm at your aunt's house right now.*

All the little buzzing happy feelings I had from taking Mags to the baby store disappear in an instant. I can't respond to the text. I can't even think about it.

I drop my phone on the side table and rub my hands over my face, trying to keep down the emotions, then turn back to look at my personal tip jar. It won't be long, if I keep saving. It's going to keep adding up, and one day I'll have enough money not to worry. I don't need to be rich. I just need to be okay.

"I *am* okay," I tell myself out loud, even as tears sting my eyes. I repeat it in my head until I believe it. I *am* okay. I have a good job and a nice place and everything I need to get back on track. I'm more than okay. And she's okay for now.

One deep breath and I'm headed for a long, hot shower. I try not to think of all the times this has happened before, and instead I focus on work. Where time goes by; I can take care of everything and everyone; the world is right; Griffin gives me those looks; and no one knows anything about what's really happening in my life.

CHAPTER 5

GRIFFIN

A few days have passed since my mom was here but with how much she texts me you'd think it's been months. I shake my head, smirking at her message and tell her I have to go; I'm working at the bar. She means well but I really do have to work, and she keeps asking me about Renee.

Fuck. I love my mom but this thing with me and Renee feels delicate, and I just don't want anyone making it more...I don't even know.

I stop thinking about it and go back to work instead, glancing up at the clock knowing her shift isn't for a little while giving me something to look forward to.

I take my time, wiping down the bottles and keeping everything pristine behind the bar—I'm at the bar for most shifts, usually, so it's business as usual. The front doors open and Robert Barnes, newly elected city manager and previous pain in my ass turned friend, walks in.

He pulls off a navy-blue hat and sticks it in his coat pocket, then shrugs off the coat, huffing and puffing the cold air away.

"Hello, Mr. City Manager, good afternoon," I call to him, smirking and taking a note of how much older he looks with his suit on. He's around my age and an all right guy once I got to know him. I've been getting to know him recently, especially late at night when the town talks about what happened with his parents.

Robert laughs a loud, deep belly laugh that fills up the whole bar. "No need to be so formal, Griff. How are you?"

"Good. How are you? Stressed out from keeping the town on the straight and narrow?" I keep it easy with him and grab an empty glass, thinking he's going to want his usual.

"Yeah." Robert hangs his coat on the back of a bar stool and slides onto it, exhaling deeply. "It's always a near thing in places like this. All kinds of shenanigans going on. The tree lighting ceremony has to be moved up half an hour because of the middle school band concert. Can you believe it?"

"I can't." I hold up the glass and he nods. "That's a hell of a conundrum," I joke as if I would have any idea, and I fill his drink up to the rim.

He laughs again and accepts his drink. "I gathered up our best and brightest and figured it out. We can't have anybody missing their kid's first trombone solo."

I think back to the few band concerts I attended when I was in middle school and make a face, which gets another laugh out of Robert. "I'd be all right if never reminded of my short stint in band."

We chat about the upcoming holidays and the events the local shops are putting on. I'll make sure the bar's open for the tree lighting. We're pretty much always open, so it won't be a problem, but maybe I could set up a mini tree in the window or on the bar. Hell, maybe we could even raise money in a tip jar for the middle school band.

Might not be a bad idea, all things considered. With the town budget being the way it is, the middle school band can probably use all the help they can get.

We're in mid-conversation after a half-hour when Renee comes in through the front door. The second the door shuts behind her, she turns her head and looks at me, and our eyes just lock. A shiver goes down my spine and the grin slips. *Something's wrong.*

I can't look away from her. She normally has a warm smile on when she's working, but today she looks a little worried, or sad, and I almost want to ask her what's going on or give her time off or pour her a drink. Renee probably wouldn't appreciate any of that, since she picks up shifts whenever she can, so instead I just stare at her like a fool not knowing what to say.

Finally she looks away. "Hey, Robert," she calls, and makes her way to the back to get set up for her shift.

When I turn back to Robert, he's grinning at me the same way my mom did. Damn it, I've been caught again, and this time it's one of the guys who literally knows everyone in town.

I clear my throat. "What's on deck for the new year, then? Big party on Main Street? Has the town invested in a ball we can drop from the second story of the bank?"

Robert huffs. "When are you going to ask her out?"

"What?" My heart beats loud in my ears and I know I've gone red in the face again. *What this woman does to me*...hell I don't know why she gets to me like she does.

"What do you mean...what?" Robert gives me a skeptical look. "I think—"

The door bangs open again, and two guys from town come inside, laughing. "Robert!" one of them calls. Once again, I'm grateful for the interruption.

I know I should stay in my spot behind the bar, but

the worried expression on Renee's face has me worried for her. If it's something I can help with, I should find out what it is. I should at least check in with her before she picks up any tables. That's just what a good boss should do, right?

"Be right back," I tell Robert and offer a short wave to the two guys who just walked in. "One second," I tell them, and they nod, smiles on their face as they chat it up with Robert.

I head to the back to the employee break room. Renee's standing at one of the cubbies, tugging on her uniform over her shirt.

She's gorgeous. Her auburn hair is pulled up in a high, sleek ponytail, and she's not wearing much makeup but enough to pink her cheeks and deepen the color of her lips. The sight of her body in the uniform as she tugs it over her waist is enough to make me hard, but I ignore it. She's gorgeous head to toe, but from the way she's standing, something's off.

"Hey."

Renee turns, her eyebrows going up. The worried expression stays on her face for a couple beats before she smiles. It's forced and fake and the sight of it makes my heart race. "Hey," she says.

"You doing okay?" I ask, keeping it light even though I'm sure she can see right through it.

"Of course." Renee flips her ponytail and gives her uniform one last tug before giving herself a once-over in the floor-to-ceiling mirror in the corner. She catches me looking in the mirror and smiles again. "Why wouldn't I be?"

I pause a beat, wondering if maybe I'm thinking too much into it. Maybe I was wrong?

I don't know what to say, because I want to say too much to her. Renee's eyes drop in the mirror. Her cheeks are flushed, and she's been inside for long enough that I know it's not just the cold.

"I like your hair like that," I say and motion to her swinging ponytail. Instantly I feel foolish. It's a freaking ponytail, man. I couldn't come up with anything better?

Renee turns around and smiles directly at me, which makes my heart race until it pounds. Her eyes are all lit up with the compliment and I don't think she's faking it anymore. It's a real smile. A warmth flows through me and I want to take her ponytail and twist it around my finger just to feel how sleek it is. I wonder if she'd laugh when I did that. Or maybe lean closer, her smile remaining until I tipped her face up so I could—

"Thank you," she says graciously and with a hint of flirtation when her eyes settle on me. There's a moment, but it ends just as quickly as it started. Then Renee's moving, approaching me slowly across the break room.

I'm in deep trouble, because nobody should look that sexy when they're wearing a waitress uniform.

She steps carefully to the side when she reaches me, but it's not as careful as I thought. It doesn't leave enough room between us, and I don't get out of the way in time, so when she passes by, her arm brushes against mine.

It's electric and the tension immediately heightens between us.

Renee stops when we make contact, taking a short breath like she just remembered something. I didn't think my heart could beat any faster, but it does. Maybe she's going to tell me what was bothering her, or maybe— I'm not sure, but she's close enough that I can smell her shampoo and a light, sweet scent that's all her. I want to lean down and breathe in so I can be sure, but I stand up tall, my body still but my heart beating a hundred miles an hour.

"You know..." Renee bites her lip and glances up at me through her lashes.

"What do I know?" I ask her, trying not to look like I'm breathing too deep. My face is definitely red. I can't deny it this time. Luckily there's nobody to see but Renee and she's blushing, too.

"I might be doing a little better now that I saw you," she says softly, just for me to hear.

A pleased feeling rushes through me. I'm even

warmer now, and it's hard to think with her so close. The way she looks into my eyes is flirtatious and teasing and yet serious at the same time.

Renee tilts her chin up a fraction of an inch. I can't move. A very small part of my head is warning me that I shouldn't have been in the break room with her for so long. I'm not supposed to be standing this close to one of my employees.

But I'm too caught in her gaze. As hers drops to my lips, mine drops to her lips. They're soft and kissable and I know they'd feel like heaven and sin all at once against mine. If I leaned down and kissed her right now, we'd still be barely touching, and then I'd have to put my hands on her waist to bring her closer. I'd finally know how her waist felt in my hands and how the rest of her body felt against mine.

It must be a thousand degrees in the break room, like the heat has kicked on full blast and it's all blowing down on us. My next thought is to strip my shirt over my head, and that leads to a long line of other thoughts that can't happen in the break room when anybody could walk in.

I could just lock the door. My mind races with what could happen between us and how quickly we could give in to temptation.

Renee breathes out and blinks, and just like that the moment is over.

I swallow thickly as she takes a half step back and we both pretend nothing happened.

"Thanks," she whispers, and then she breaks away, her ponytail swinging in the air behind her. I let out a breath I didn't know I was holding, and then her footsteps are headed out the door and to the front as she starts her shift.

For a minute I don't move at all. A steadying breath in and a steadying breath out are all I'm left with. She was close enough for me to kiss her, thanking me for making her feel better, and I didn't say anything.

"Damn it," I say to the empty room, then shake off the tension in my shoulders. There's no way I can go out front without taking a few minutes to settle down, so I leave the break room and head to the office in the back. Once I'm inside, I shut the door behind me and throw myself into the chair by the desk.

I can't physically kick myself when I'm sitting in a chair, but if I could, I would. The chair creaks under me as I rock back, breathing hard at how badly I've just screwed up. What was I thinking back there?

That was my shot, wasn't it? Renee opened the door for me. She was flirting with me. She stood there for so long I could have kissed her ten times over, and I didn't do anything, because I didn't know what she'd think of it afterward. I wasn't sure if it was the right place or the right time, but who cares? I had a chance and instead of taking it—

I just clammed up and stared at her.

And now Renee's long gone, out in the front picking up tables, and it's too late to get that moment back. I run my hand down my face and think it's probably best. I'm her boss and there's no going back from that first kiss.

I lean back in the chair and realize one of these days I don't think I'm going to be able to stop myself. And when that happens, we'll both be screwed.

CHAPTER 6

RENEE

What the hell is wrong with me? I almost kissed my boss in the break room. I stare at the spot in wonder, like I've done every day since it happened. That would-be kiss is all I can think about. It's all I *want* to think about.

Actually, I think Griffin almost kissed me. We both almost kissed each other. I don't think I'd be able to say who started it, because if he *did* kiss me I wouldn't be able to think of anything else at all.

My heart beats fast and for three days afterward I imagine what would have happened. What would it be like to get lost in his touch?

Every time I stop thinking about Griffin looking at me with those dark brown eyes, his breathing short, and his face flushed, something reminds me of him. The bar. The barstools. The booths. Any random doorway can remind me of that moment, and then I'm right back there, imagining what would've happened if I'd gotten up on tiptoes and given him a kiss instead of just hoping he'd kiss me.

As the sun sets and the snow falls behind the lone window in the break room, I get lost in that moment all over again. I wish he would have done it.

A patron calling out, "night!" from the bar snaps me back to the present. I'm pretty sure he was the last customer here and I'm quick to retie my apron.

It's a pretty slow night, even for December. I'd guess that's because of the weather. There's light snowfall outside, and it might snow more, so I don't think many people will be out tonight.

It never snows in Beaufort. That's what people say. They mean it rarely snows here. One of the TVs behind the bar is showing a weather report. They're calling for an inch or two, so nobody's going to risk driving.

I watch the snow fall for a little while longer. It's beautiful because it's rare, and I want to take advantage of the view. If it snows three more times this winter we'll be lucky.

A door in the back closes, and the sound of footsteps makes me turn around. Instantly my heart pounds in that excited way. Like it's been waiting for a redo as much as I have.

Griffin comes out from the office in back, looking toward the window with his eyebrows raised. He looks at the snow for a few beats, too, then moves over to the bar and leans on it. His lips are slightly parted, and I can't stop staring.

"I wonder if we should close up early so we don't get snowed in." He swallows, the cords in his neck tightening, as he slips his hands into his jean pockets. He looks relaxed but also not.

Like he's tense but only because he's ready for what's to come.

My boss glances at me like I'll have the answer.

The only answer I can think of is to lean on the bar like he is. We're separated by a few feet of wood and paneling, but our hands are an inch apart. He's so close that I can smell his cologne. His broad shoulders and rough stubble only make him look more attractive.

"I don't know," I say finally, licking my lower lip. "Can you get snowed in because of two inches of snow?"

My head says no, but I guess you never know. Most people in Beaufort don't know what to do if it snows, so maybe it's possible that you could get trapped in a bar from snow that doesn't reach your ankles.

Griffin's eyes drop to my lips. "Hmm. I think it depends on how good your tires are," he says almost absently.

I know a man talking about car tires shouldn't be sexy in any way, but Griffin says it like he'd say *I want to strip that shirt right off you* or *do you know how beautiful you'd look naked* or *I could lick you all night long.*

A blush rises up my cheeks but it's the kind of blush that hits all over.

I couldn't care less about tires or snow. All I want is to kiss him. Just to escape into his arms and leave the hard parts of my life behind.

If I did that, I could forget about everything and just kiss him like nothing in the world mattered except feeling his lips on mine. I could be the person who's got her life together and has everything she's ever wanted, at least for a few minutes.

I clear my throat as more heat pours into my face. It's a good thing the lights are dim.

I finally answer him. "Well, I don't know anything about tires or if mine are any good, but I think tonight it might be best to get out of here."

Griffin hasn't moved from his spot on the bar. He looks deep into my eyes, and I remember the break room. The moment goes on and on until my heart is hammering in my chest, and I can barely breathe.

"Yeah," Griffin agrees gruffly. "Let's close this place down."

It's been slow enough that most of the closing duties are done already. Griffin flips the chairs onto the tables, and I run a broom and a mop over the floor one more time. One more round of dishes set to dry for tomorrow, cash settled in the register, and that's it. Griffin goes to the front door and flips the switch for the open sign while I head to the back to change out of my uniform.

He's waiting for me when I come back out with my coat and purse over my arm. Griffin taps his keys against his thigh. They clink together and it sounds loud in the silence of this closed-down bar.

"Is there anything else you need before I head home?" I ask. I feel almost naked without my uniform, like he can see through my loose sweater and all the way to my racing heart.

Griffin doesn't answer at first. "Nothing for the bar, no. Do you want me to drop you off? I'd be happy to do it if you don't want to drive in the snow."

I laugh at him, which sounds even louder than the keys. "I can drive just fine."

Griffin shrugs, a smile lighting up his face and fading away. "I know you don't need any help. I was just trying to be a gentleman."

Griffin Matthews, ever the gentleman. Something slips in my chest and clicks into place as I stare back at him. I'm the one who's not being very ladylike, because I can't help it when my eyes drop down to his lips. I just can't stop wondering what it would be like. You can't stand that close to a man like him without wondering what it would be like to kiss him. To wonder if it would last forever.

"You look like you want to kiss me," Griffin says softly, in a gruff tone that tells me he's thinking un-gentlemanly like thoughts just as I am.

"Do I?" A small smile creeps up on my face as I tease him.

Griffin nods and smiles too.

I take a steadying breath, because if I don't say something now, I'll regret it. There's no better time than this. The bar's closed, everybody's at home because of the snow, and we can do anything we want, at least for tonight.

"Want to pretend you're not my boss?" I ask, matching his tone. "So I could just kiss you and finally know what that feels like?" The moment the words are out of my mouth, I can't believe I said them. I can't believe I'd risk the one place in my life where I have stability. And the one person I could live my entire life watching, knowing he's happy with how I'm doing.

Griffin looks at me, and for once there's nobody to interrupt. The tension between us crackles through the air.

"Have you been wondering?" he asks, taking a single step forward.

"Yeah," I admit as my heartbeat gets louder in my ears.

There's another short silence, and Griffin walks forward slowly until he's a foot away from me. It's so much warmer in the air when he's standing close.

"I could pretend that, if you can pretend you're not my employee."

"I'm not. Not right now. I'm just a girl who wandered into the bar and saw something she liked."

"What was that?" he questions.

"You." I take another deep breath. "I've been interested for a while now, and I need something to take the edge off."

His eyes narrow just slightly and I second guess what I said. "Just a kiss from someone I saw across the room."

"I'm a gentleman," he repeats, and puts his hands at my waist. His touch is steady and warm, and I want to fall into him. "It wouldn't be right to let you leave without giving you what you need."

"It wouldn't be right at all," I say softly, lost in his longing gaze.

"Kiss me then," he murmurs just beneath his breath.

"Just like you want to."

"What about you?" I ask. I'm suddenly nervous now that I'm so close to him again. I know he wants this too, otherwise he wouldn't be touching me. But I have to be sure. "Has this been on your mind?"

"On my mind?" he questions and then huffs a laugh. "I've been pretending I'm not your boss and wondering what it would be like to kiss you...because I saw something I want, too."

"Just one kiss?" I ask, not knowing how I could stand the tension for this long.

"As many as you want," he answers.

And then I do it. I get up on my tiptoes, but before I can kiss him, he leans down and kisses me first. It's magic and surreal and everything I dreamed it would be. His lips are exactly as soft as I thought they'd be, and he kisses me confidently. Griffin moves his hands up my body to my neck and he cups my face, then threads his fingers through my hair and deepens the kiss.

His touch is hot and heady, and I'm dizzy with lust. I want more with every fraction of a second that passes.

I moan into his mouth, and I think he makes a sound into mine. I can't tell because he's pushing my coat and purse to the floor and taking me in his arms. I can't help myself. I go for everything I want and need, my hands slipping up his jacket, needing skin on skin. Griffin kisses down my neck while he unbuttons my pants and pushes at them until I can kick them off. I climb right up into his arms and wrap my legs around his waist, and then he carries me to the bar.

It all happens so fast, and I do everything I can not to think and to just focus on the moment. So I can remember this forever.

Somehow he manages to strip off his outer shirt and lay it down, then perches me on top of it so my bare ass doesn't get cold. Griffin unzips his jeans with frantic motions while I kiss the corner of his mouth and his neck. His scent is intoxicating. Hell, I could be drunk right now and my mind wouldn't know the difference. I'm drunk on him and the idea of giving in after all this time. I don't want to let go of him, so I throw my arms around his neck and balance on the bar.

He takes his dick in his hand and runs the tip of his cock between my slit, letting out a loud groan. *Tease.* He teases me and I let my head fall back, feeling the cool air against my hot face.

"That's so good," he says under his breath and then runs opened mouth kisses down my throat. "Damn, that's so good." My nipples pebble as the back of his knuckle brushes against them. "So fucking beautiful, my little tease," he says and presses in just slightly deeper.

I can't stand it. "I need you," I whimper, and he catches

my "please" with his lips, kissing me more fervently.

I move my hips to get him closer and he pushes inside me. In a single swift moment my lips fall as I gasp silently. He's big, but I don't have to brace against it—I'm already wet from the kiss and from wanting him so badly for so long. His girth stretches me with a slight sting of pain that quickly turns to pleasure. He strums my clit and I writhe against him until his thrusts are deeper and in a steady pace. My toes curl and I cry out his name.

"Holy fuck, Griffin," I moan, and he fucks me harder and deeper in response.

Then his hands go back to my hips, and I lean more of my weight on him. "So close...I'm so close." My breath is loud in my ears, and his lips are hot on my neck.

It's fast and frantic. I'm barely aware that I'm half naked on the bar not just kissing Griffin, but getting fucked by him like that's been his fantasy all this time.

Griffin moves his hips and hits the perfect spot, making me moan out loud. I can't help myself. He holds me closer to his body to get more contact between us and I can feel my orgasm building up and up between my legs.

He leans his head closer to my ear and murmurs, "That's it, baby. Come all over me. Give it to me, you little tease."

That pushes me over the edge. Griffin keeps talking

while I ride out the pleasure, though I don't understand a single thing he's saying. Aftershocks go through me as he holds me as close as he can and grinds into me, breathing fast. His breath stutters as he starts to come and Griffin kisses me again, the deepest kiss we've shared so far.

And then it breaks. And then it's over. And then it all hits me at once.

What the hell did I just do?

CHAPTER 7

GRIFFIN

It takes me a long time to fall asleep after I get home from the bar because I can't stop thinking about her. I should feel more conflicted about the fact that I just had sex with my employee, but I can't. I don't feel guilty at all. It felt so fucking right. She felt right.

And when she stepped down off that bar and let me help her get her clothes back on, she gave me that look. I fucking love that look on her. Like she wants nothing more than for me to tell her what a good girl she is.

It was Renee's idea to pretend and exactly what I wanted, but the second we agreed on it, that was my new reality. I know it sounds crazy, but my whole life disappeared. We were just two people who met in a bar and had to have each other. Nothing's wrong with that.

Nothing was wrong with driving her home afterward, either, except that I wanted to invite her to my place and keep her in my bed all night. My little tease is stubborn, but she wants me just like I want her and that's all I need right now.

My alarm wakes me up early the next morning. I'm tired as fuck but excited for the day. I don't remember the last time I got out of bed with this much excitement. Outside the street lights are just starting to turn on and everything is covered in a thin layer of snow.

I brush my teeth, holding back a smile remembering last night, and throw on a pair of shorts and an old tee shirt I work out in, then head down to the gym I set up in my basement. I practically jog down the stairs thinking about her soft moans and just how fucking good she felt. I can't stop thinking about her and the fact that we finally went for it. She was worth the wait. Worth every fucking second just for last night. I flick the fluorescent lights on and stretch out my shoulders.

It's not a huge space down here, but I put a decent amount of work into it after I moved in. It was a dusty, old, unfinished basement but laminate floors, a bit of drywall, and paint made a huge difference. I used the leftover paneling from the bar, and I've got a set of weights and a treadmill. I spend ten minutes or so warming up and checking out the snow. The basement is a walkout with a sliding door so it doesn't feel like I'm in a cave.

It's still early, so I start lifting, trying to complete as many reps as possible before I break down and text Renee. I debate on exactly what to say with every rep.

I fucking hope she loved it as much as I did.

Finally, not able to resist any longer, I set down my heaviest dumbbell and grab my phone. It takes several tries to write out the message. I don't want to screw this up.

Griffin: *I really enjoyed last night*

I second guess the message as soon as I hit send, but there's no way to stop it. Renee's phone has already lit up with my name on it. Staring at the screen, I wait and wait and then glance at the dumbbells...as if I can distract myself while I wait.

I pace around the basement with my hands on my head, then go back to the weights and concentrate hard on my next set. Thinking about good form doesn't do anything to keep my mind off her, though.

Renee's in my head. I've never felt like this about anyone. Hell, I can't remember a time I texted a girl I hooked up with and then wondered if she'd text me back. I can't believe the way I feel about her is this strong already. My heart beats faster when I think about anything related to her. Every time I turn my head toward the window and see the snow, I'm right back there in the bar with my lips on hers and her body wrapped around mine.

Anxiousness builds at the memory: I fucked her on the bar. My employee.

And I'd do it again, if she looked at me with those eyes and asked me to pretend I'm not her boss. I wouldn't even have to think about it.

The weights drop to the cushioned mat with a loud thunk as I glance at my phone again. No reply yet. I shake off the tension; she's probably still sleeping. Hell it's early and I'd rather still be in bed, too.

If this were anybody else I would have texted Brody about it already. I probably would've talked to him a long time ago. I switch to another set of weights and think back on all the times I've called him in the middle of the night about one thing or another or pulled him aside to ask him what he thought.

I can't tell Brody though if this is a onetime thing. If she wants this to stay on the down low, I'm more than willing. Brody would tell Mags in a heartbeat. I know he would. So I don't trust telling him a damn thing just yet.

It doesn't feel like a onetime thing to me. I stand up straighter, stretching my arms above my head and take a few deep breaths. Last night felt like *more*, but was that part of the pretending? Was it just because we had to close the bar and it was snowing in Beaufort and that never happens? Was it because she came into work feeling down and needed a pick-me-up?

Nerves settle in my stomach, and I ignore them. I work through my routine while it gets brighter outside and I wait for my phone to go off. It feels like forever when it finally does.

I force myself to finish the set and catch my breath before I take my phone off the windowsill and check the message. It could be from Brody or Patty or anybody else who works at the bar, calling in sick or asking whether the hours are different today because of the snow. It could be my mom checking up on me. I brace myself for it not to be Renee.

Renee: *I liked it too*

Fuck yeah. I punch my fist in the air in victory. All that worrying for nothing. I will never understand how she keeps me on edge like she does.

I reread her message and then debate on what else to say. I have to do another few laps around my basement to calm down. My heart is pumping hard, and I know it's a combo of that woman and the workout.

Part of me wants to text her back right this second, but I make myself wait. It's almost certain that it's obvious how much I'm into her. I don't want to be too forward or seem too clingy, and I need a minute to think about how I want this conversation to go, so I do a few more reps.

When I glance at my phone again, there are bubbles on the screen like she's typing something out.

I do another rep while I stare at it. The bubbles go away, then come back again. They stay on the screen for another minute after that, then disappear again.

My brow creases and I wonder what she's going to say. Then I huff out a laugh, she has me so worked up. I bet she fucking loves that. Groaning out another rep I wait and then wait some more.

I go through another full set before I let myself check for new messages.

She didn't send anything.

I have no idea what that's supposed to mean. She did all that typing and didn't send anything?

Those nerves riddle their way up again, but I shove them down. Back to the weights. I pick up a set, determined to finish what I started, trying not to get in my head over a text.

A cold sweat breaks out over my shoulders as I push myself even harder. Determined to finish strong and then text her the first fucking thing that comes to my mind.

I want you again.

I'm glad you enjoyed it too.

Next time maybe we should try a bed.

I smirk at the last thought and exhale a deep steadying breath.

I finish my set and pick up my phone. My heart pounds like it did when I signed the paperwork to buy the bar, only a hundred times harder. I'm more nervous than I ever was in high school when homecoming and prom were the events of the year. In fact nothing in high school ever felt this intense, but in a good way. I have to follow that feeling.

And I have to do it now, because Renee's not scheduled to work the next two days, and I can't stand waiting that long.

Griffin: *Want to go bowling or something?*

Tossing down the phone I grab a towel to wipe off but keep my eyes on the screen.

There's another minute of silence from Renee. I use the time to run a sanitizing wipe over my weights. I flip off the basement lights and climb the stairs, towel over my shoulder, then stand in front of the fridge and fill a glass with chilled water.

I'm drinking it when my phone goes off.

Renee: *That might look like a date, and this is just pretend, right?*

My whole body heats up and my heart rate picks

right back up. The time we spent at the bar last night repeats in my head, and I'm hard in no time.

This is just pretend, right?

Setting the glass down, I stare at the text. I don't know what to respond, because I don't know if this is a test or not. Does she want me to say it is pretend? Or does she want me to say I don't want it to be pretend?

At this point I just want more of her. Whether that's hooking up in secret or going out on dates. Whatever she wants, I want. So I decide to tell her just that.

Griffin: *Well what is it that you want? I'm fine with whatever you'd like*

Her response is instant.

Renee: *Why don't you take me to the drive-in movie theater?*

Okay, that's definitely a date, even if we pretend that it's not. No one in town sees. We get to take it slow. I'm down for that. Nodding my head as I type I agree.

Griffin: *Hell yeah I'll take you to the drive-in movie*

Renee: *Cool :) Tell me when.*

Before I can look at my schedule and reply she messages again.

Renee: *Have you looked at the snow this morning? It might be the prettiest snow I've ever seen*

I smile down at the screen.

Some of my nervousness fades away. I put down the

phone, stretch my arms over my head, and take another look at the snow outside my house. It's pretty, but nowhere near as pretty as Renee. I catch myself smiling at the memory of how gorgeous she was last night, before and after she was naked on that bar, which is a clear sign that I'm stuck on this girl. I decide to be cheesy and this time I don't worry about it at all. I'm sure she'll tease me over it, and I'll enjoy that too.

Griffin: *I did, it's not as pretty as you*

CHAPTER 8

RENEE

It's snug and warm under my blanket on the couch in my apartment, and I know I should get up and get going. I don't have work today, but there are things I could get done around the apartment. And sitting here, just letting my mind wander isn't doing me any good. I keep finding myself biting my nails. It's a bad habit to kick.

I could bundle up and go for a walk in the snow. I could journal and try to figure out where I'm at in terms of my goals.

But I can't do anything, because my mind is just a blank buzz. I'm going back and forth between feeling amazing about last night, like I got something I wanted and got away with it and everything is *fine...*

And feeling like I ruined everything.

I don't know what to think but having a fling with my boss is not at all going to end well. I know exactly how this story ends and I can't believe I let myself fall for him.

I don't want to be stuck on the couch all day, so I get up and get myself another cup of coffee. In slippers and my favorite nightie and matching robe, I try my best not to think the worst. It's hard not to though when I know I never should have done that last night. The coffee machine gives a soothing hum as I look out the apartment's windows at the snow that's fallen all over the rooftops of the houses across the street. I try to remind myself that a few minutes ago I was smiling at Griffin's cheesy joke rather than thinking the worst of the worst.

I can't panic about this. I *liked* what happened last night. I might have even loved it. I've wanted to kiss Griffin for so long, and all the stars just happened to align, so it can't be a bad thing that I took a chance, right?

It might be a bad thing in the long run. Unless we just keep it a secret.

I sip at my caramel coffee in a bright pink mug with white daisies and go round and round in my head until

I can't stand it anymore, then pick up my phone and text Mags.

Renee: *I think I might have messed up something*

Mags texts me back within thirty seconds before I'm even able to put my phone down. The nerves prick at the ends of my fingertips.

Mags: *What happened?*

I start to answer her, but I don't know how to explain that I wouldn't have tried to kiss Griffin, except I felt like there would never be another chance. It never snows in Beaufort.

It's so silly but all I could think is that if it's snowing maybe I'm dreaming, and if I am it's okay. I'm allowed to go for it then. The real world can't hurt me if it's just pretend.

I don't get away with spending all this time not answering. My phone rings a second later and I answer it as I make my way back to the warm spot on the sofa.

"Hey." I rub my forehead and pull the blankets tighter around my lap. "Sorry for texting you this early."

Mags snorts. "It's not that early, but you can't leave me on a cliffhanger like that."

"Sorry for that, too." I pick at an invisible thread on the blanket and try to gather my thoughts.

"What happened? Is it your mom?"

"Not this time..."

I take a sip of my coffee just to buy some time. I can tell by the silence on the phone that Mags is waiting patiently for me to speak, but she's not going to let me off the hook.

I clear my throat. "Last night at the bar." I start but I can't keep going. We've been friends for as long as I can remember. Mags knows. She knows everything.

"You were working last night, right?"

"Yeah. I was working. I guess this story started a few days ago."

"I'm settling in," Mags says. I can hear some movement in the background of the call. "Okay, tell me what happened a few days ago."

"I went in for my shift and I was feeling down about everything. You know?"

"I know," she answers with genuine concern.

"I just couldn't shake it, and Griffin could tell." I can still picture him staring at me in the break room, standing so still, and how much I regretted not kissing him after. It would have been so easy. "Anyway, he came into the break room to check on me, and—"

"And you two made out," Mags says decisively.

I laugh. "No. But there was some...tension."

"Sexual tension," she says, still every bit as decisive as she was before and a bit more upbeat now. Her ease helps me relax a touch and I'm able to spit it out.

"I guess you could call it that, yes. We were standing very close to one another. I thought about kissing him, but I didn't."

Mags groans. "What a bummer…"

"We were at work," I point out. "My head has been a mess with everything, and I had to get to my shift, and if anybody had walked in on us-—"

"I get it," Mags says. "So then what happened?"

"I worked my shift and caught him looking at me a few times, but that's normal." We both laugh at my little joke. I'm more than aware that Griffin is into me. And for a while I was into the idea of him. But reality has a way of reminding me why I can't have a relationship.

As her laughter tapers off, I watch the sun on the snow. It's melting fast, and it's so pretty before everyone drives all over it and turns it into dirty slush.

"Okay," Mags says. "Sorry. I just know he's into you, so it makes sense that he stares at you at work all the time."

"He doesn't stare at me at work *all* the time." My face gets hot. "Like, there have been a few times when there's—"

"Tension?" Mags says with a laugh in her voice.

"Fine. Yes. But it's not like he spends all day watching me. He's professional. I'm professional."

A gust of wind blows across my lone living room window, making a soft rattling sound. It's not snowing anymore, and I bet what's on the ground will be gone by tomorrow.

"Back to last night, then. You screwed up being professional?"

"Kind of?" I bite my lip, thinking of how to tell her the story, which usually means I'm overthinking it. "Griffin was thinking we should close the bar early because of the snow. You know how people are. It was empty. Nobody wanted to drive."

"I didn't want to drive," Mags says.

"We figured nobody else would be coming in. So we closed the place up, and I went to the back room to get my stuff, and when I came out, he was standing there."

The way Griffin looked at me still gives me the good kind of shivers. I have to close my eyes at the memory. I just wanted to feel for a moment what it would be like. My head pounds with last night's mistake and Mags gets impatient.

"Is *that* when you finally made out with him?"

It's my turn to laugh. "No. He asked me if I wanted him to drive me home, and I said no, that kind of thing, and then he said...you look like you want to kiss me."

"Because you *did* want to kiss him."

"Yeah, and nobody can blame me." I tip my head back on the arm of the couch and close my eyes. "My best friend isn't going to blame me, I hope."

"I could never blame you," Mags says earnestly. "He's good looking. I'm allowed to say that because it's objectively true."

"So then I kissed him." My heart races at the memories of how quickly the kiss had turned passionate, like we both knew we'd only have the one chance. It seemed almost like a spell that would be over the second we left the bar. "And then some."

Mags squeals so loud that I have to hold the phone away from my ear.

"Oh my God, Renee." I can almost see her with her hand on her chest and her face all red from being so excited for me. "Finally."

I'm not sure what to say to that, but I can't say nothing to Mags. She always knows when I'm staying quiet because I'm conflicted.

"Renee," she says, quieter. "Did you not have a good time?"

"I had a *great* time." I let out a groan. "I just don't know if..." I can't finish but luckily Mags takes over with an interrogation.

"Well, if you didn't have a bad time—are you telling me you did it, like, in the office? Or—"

"On the bar," I say in a small voice.

"That's so hot," Mags whispers. "I can't believe you went for it...like went for it."

I glance around my neat, inexpensive apartment. It's mostly filled with simple build-your-own furniture and pops of colors in pillows and throws.

"He texted me this morning and asked if I wanted to go bowling."

"A bowling date? That is so cute."

"I turned him down."

"*What*? You did not turn him down. You've had a crush on him for like forever."

My stomach sinks. Mags knows about my home life. She knows about what's going on with my mother. She knows more than everyone else how right now is not a good time. And with my boss? If something were to happen and I lost that job, there's so much that could go wrong so quickly. I try to keep it simple, rather than letting the emotions show in my voice.

"I've thought he was hot for forever, but I can't date him, Mags! I work for him. We can't go on dates or the whole town will have something to say about it."

She's silent for a beat, and my heart aches. Mags understands what it's like to have the whole town weigh in on something that should be your own personal decision.

"I hope I didn't hurt your feelings. I'm really sorry if I did," I tell her.

"You didn't," she says, "But how could bowling go

badly? Unless you dropped the ball on your foot or got it stuck to your fingers and he had to take you to the ER. But even that would be kind of romantic."

"It's not romantic to drop a bowling ball on your foot," I point out. "And I'm saying my job could go badly, and I need my job." I feel anxious thinking about having to quit or getting fired because Griffin changes his mind about me, or the town puts pressure on him for dating an employee. So many things could happen. "I would be really screwed if I lost my job."

"You're not going to lose your job if you go bowling."

"I suggested that he take me to the drive-in movie instead."

Mags huffs a laugh. "Perfect time for a drive-in movie. You'll have to stay cuddled up in the car, since it'll be freezing the whole time."

I love Mags, I always have, but she doesn't really seem to be getting it. Maybe my silence is a clue to her that I'm not convinced this is a good thing.

"I vote take it slow and easy and try not to worry. I think this could be a good thing," she says with an upbeat tone. "I really do Renee. I think you have a lot on your mind right now and there's a time and a place to worry, but this could be a good thing. Just...maybe let it happen and see where life takes you," she suggests, but it doesn't ease a darn thing for me. I know where life goes the moment I start to think it's going to be okay. Miss happily ever after forgets what happened the last time I thought I could fall in love...

I sigh out loud. "Listen, I left my car at the bar. Can you drive me over in a little bit so I can get it?"

"Of course. Did Griffin take you home last night?"

"Yeah," I answer, picking at my nails and then remembering the drive home last night. "He was really nice."

"Oh my God," Mags breathes, and there's a quiet *thump* as she falls back onto her couch or the pillows on her bed. "That is so sweet and romantic."

I laugh at her, feeling extremely fond of my best friend. But not at all at ease at the idea of letting whatever is going to happen, happen. I thought she would understand but she doesn't. She starts talking about the two of us falling in love and getting caught kissing behind the bar but making it seem like it would be some love story rather than a town scandal.

"Your pregnancy hormones are showing, Mags."

Mags laughs, "You're right, but there's nothing I can do about that now. Give me fifteen minutes and I'll come pick you up."

"Thanks Mags." I tell her before hanging up, "Love you."

"Love you too. Try not to worry. It's okay," she says in a tone that reminds me she does know what I'm feeling.

"I promise you it's going to be okay."

I can't say anything in response to that. Mags should know better than to make promises she can't keep.

CHAPTER 9

GRIFFIN

With the din of chatter at the bar, I sit restlessly at the booth in the back, not able to focus on anything. I don't want to bother Renee on her days off, so I don't text her the next day, but I keep checking to see if she texts me. We settled on the weekend for our not-date movie night as she put it. If that's what she wants to call it and she wants a more casual thing, I'm fine with that. Still can't get her out of my head though.

Brody's heavy exhale reminds me that we're both staring at paperwork. He's actually working on finances and I'm...staring at the same page on this stack that I was ten minutes ago.

I have a blue pen and Brody has a red pen. There are very, very few pages that have been marked with blue.

"Spill it," he says, his eyes boring into me. With a clean shave and a polo, he seems more like himself.

"Spill what?" I look at him with as close as I can get to a straight face, though my pulse is racing from how blunt he was. I can't exactly look innocent, because I can't get Renee off my mind, and I can't pretend there's nothing going on. Still, it takes me by surprise, and I wasn't ready to *spill,* as Brody says.

He furrows his forehead. "Whatever you're thinking about. You've been jiggling your foot for twenty minutes and it's driving me fucking insane."

"It's nothing." I plant both feet on the floor and look down at the printed-out spreadsheets. "I'll tell you about it later."

"So it's not nothing then." Brody tosses his pen down on the table, clearly ready to ignore the rest of the financials until he has the answers he wants. "Tell me now so we can get back to running our business without me being distracted by you being distracted."

My best friend sits back in the booth and crosses his arms over his chest, looking me up and down. I don't like that look. "This about Renee?"

Fucking hell. How does he know?

With a quick inhale I readjust in my seat, not saying a word at first.

"Come on. Out with it," he urges.

I rub my hands over my face, let out a sigh, and say, "Yeah, it's about Renee."

"Jesus, finally." Brody slaps his hand down on the table. "I thought I was going to be a grandfather by the time you made your move."

I give him a look.

"So...you did right? You asked her out?"

"Well, I made a move."

Brody leans forward, looking at me like I've never told him anything more exciting in both our lives. "What kind of move was it? After-work drinks? Did you run into her in the grocery store? Oh, shit, the snow—did her car get stuck?"

"Her car didn't get stuck in two inches of snow. And it was after work, technically. But we didn't have drinks."

He gestures with his hands for me to continue when I pause, not knowing what exactly to tell. "What *did* you do?"

She didn't say not to tell anyone, but it's obvious she wants this to be a quiet thing. I struggle to know where the line is. I just look at him. I've known Brody for so long now that most times we don't have to say everything out loud. He narrows his eyes, and then they get big, and I nod.

He whistles quietly, although I catch a few glances from the two men at the bar. He leans back in his seat again, a grin plastered on his face. "So you're seeing each other?"

"Not exactly." I give him a vague outline of how it went down and how my text conversation with Renee went yesterday. "So now we have plans to go to the drive-in movie theater."

Brody laughs. "Of course you would take her to the drive-in movie theater."

"It was her idea," I bark back with a smile. "I get the feeling she just wants to keep it quiet, you know?"

Brody's eyes narrow but he nods his head like he understands. "Like how quiet?"

"Like I don't think she wants me telling anyone, including you."

He reaches for his beer and takes a swig. It's a fresh batch and I'm damn proud of it. He grins into the glass while tasting it before squaring his shoulders and nodding more confidently.

"Small towns talk, and she wants to make sure there's something there before going official...I get that," he says easily, and I agree with him.

"That's probably all it is. Just her wanting to test the waters before everyone else makes a big deal out of it," I tell him even though I don't quite believe what I'm saying. Something feels off, but I shake it off. With Renee, I have a tendency to overthink things and right now, I'm grateful for whatever I can get with her. "Time will tell, and I just want to let whatever's going to happen, happen, you know?"

He lifts his beer and says, "Cheers to that."

Our glasses clink easily enough and finally I can focus on the damn spreadsheets.

ONE DAY LATER

Two days has never felt so long. I find myself staring at the clock knowing I'm finally going to see her, and I'll get a better read on what's going on between us today. I can't help the smile that comes to my face when she walks in for her shift. I caved in yesterday and sent her a couple of messages, just asking about the time she wants to go to the movies and what one she wants to see, but she only gave me one-word answers. She's playing hard to get.

My little tease.

The first thing I see is her smile. It widens when her eyes reach mine and that beautiful blush hits her cheeks.

Everything inside me warms and the anxiousness leaves in an instant. She's in her typical work attire. Black jeans and her Iron Brewery maroon sweatshirt.

Mary Sue walks in right after her and I'm careful not to show too much as I'm worried she'll be able to read it on my face just like Brody did. I do my best not to stare and instead offer Renee a "good morning," to which she laughs and rolls her eyes. "It's afternoon but good morning to you too."

We both laugh as she walks past me to get to the back room and everything feels right. Her smile does that to me.

It's Thursday and a little bit slow, so when Mary Sue leaves it's just Renee and I working. I stand behind the bar and pour drinks while she waits tables. All the while my heart races, waiting for a moment when there's no one left but just us two. When all of the food is out and Renee's done a lap of the bar to make sure everything's in shape, she comes back behind the bar with me and catches her breath.

The tension between us crackles in a good way. Like we know a secret no one else does. My smile widens when she peeks up at me through her lashes and those beautiful eyes hold a flirtation I'm now used to.

Her hands stay on the bar on either side of her as she leans against it. I'm instantly reminded of how I took her right there a few nights ago.

"How are things back here?" she asks. "You doing all right?"

I gesture to all the empty bar stools. "I don't think I'll make it. Way too busy."

Renee laughs, and the sweet sound makes me hot and bothered. What is it about her? There's just something I can't get enough of when it comes to her. The bar's not full, but it's not empty, either. That means there's no kissing allowed on this shift, and I have to remind myself of that.

Wiping down the bar, I gather up the courage to ask her something, "Hey, Renee."

She turns toward me at the sound of her name, her eyebrows raised with curiosity and her gorgeous eyes bright.

"Yes?" Renee asks and I realize I've been staring at her lips. Her cheeks are pink, so she noticed I was staring, and I still can't bring myself to look away.

"You want to come to Christmas dinner with me?" The second the invitation is out of my mouth I realize just how *not-on-the-down-low* that invitation is.

Renee blinks, and then her face speeds through about ten different emotions in a row. I'm not sure which one her face settles on in the end. She takes a small step toward me and pats the pocket of her uniform, where she keeps her bill holder and a few pens.

"Christmas dinner?" she repeats, then looks into my eyes again and lowers her voice. "That seems serious."

I could be her fake non-boss from the other night. I don't see why it has to be more complicated than that if Renee doesn't want it to be. It feels pretty complicated, though. My stomach flips over. I know she wants to take it slow, and Christmas is weeks away, so we've got time.

"I just remembered you told me once that you don't really do things for the holidays, so I wanted to offer... in case you wanted to do something and get away." Her eyes catch mine and there's a vulnerability there. It reminds me of the other night.

I shrug, acting like I'm not nervous as hell. "You can be my fake date," I offer. I don't want to agree with her that it's serious cause it's not. It's just a night back home in my small town and I think she'd like to get out of here and see where I'm from.

I go back and forth between thinking there's a real connection between us and not; I can't tell if she's playing around or not.

Renee laughs again and checks her tables, shaking her head slightly. "You haven't even taken me to the movies yet, but you want me to meet your mother?"

She sounds like she's teasing, so I give her a look that gets another laugh out of her. I could get addicted to doing that. Maybe I'm already addicted.

"One, you've already met my mother, and two, we're doing the movies this weekend," I say. "It's weeks between now and Christmas. Just wanted to invite you so you know...you don't have to decide just now."

Renee chuckles. She's blushing harder than she was before and still smiling when she looks at the bar. Renee shifts her weight from foot to foot, then pats her uniform pocket again. That means she's about to head back to her tables, who probably don't even need anything yet.

"I told my mom I'd bring someone," I lie to her. "So if you could plan on being my fake date, that could maybe be fun," I tell her and then swallow down my nerves.

"Please?" I beg, doing my best to sound like I'm mostly teasing too.

Renee glances at me, and then she steps back to the register so that my body is between her and the rest of the bar. She's as close as she was in the break room. If anybody looks too hard, they'll see us standing like this. My heart races, because this is a much riskier thing to do than pretend not to be my employee.

"I'll come with you to Christmas dinner," she agrees in a low voice. "I do have to leave early today, though. I called Patty to cover the rest of my shift. If that's okay?"

"That's fine." I can't keep the smile off my face. "Leave early if you need to."

Renee smiles back at me with a tempting look and leans forward to whisper, "Look at me. Already getting perks from fake dating my boss."

The low, sweet tone of her voice makes my cock so fucking hard so fast that I'm short of breath and lightheaded from all the blood moving to my dick so damn fast.

She smirks at me and then bites down onto her lower lip. Oh she knows exactly what she's doing. It takes everything in me to stand perfectly still and keep my hands gripping the edge of the bar top.

I can feel the rest of the bar behind us with people chatting at their tables and the music playing at the perfect volume for the afternoon. A guy at one of the tables laughs, but Renee doesn't look away from me. She's caught in my stare and waiting for a reaction.

"Yeah," I say. "I guess you are my little tease."

"Thank you," she whispers, and then she walks toward the back, glancing back at me like she wants me to follow. She makes it past the swinging door and I'm barely though when she lifts up on tiptoes and nudges her nose against mine. Renee brushes a kiss to my lips, and it takes all my concentration not to put my hands on her waist and pull her in close so I can feel her.

She gives me another soft kiss, and I kiss her back, deepening it. I let a rough groan leave my chest, more than aware that if someone came through that door we'd be caught in the act. I let myself taste her one more time and then straighten up.

She doesn't say anything, only stares up at me like she has something to say but doesn't. The blush settles into her cheeks and looks damn good. Fuck, I wish we weren't working right now 'cause I know just what she needs. She takes a second to adjust her uniform, then steps around me to head back.

"Hey, Renee?" somebody at one of her tables says the moment she walks out in front of me. "I'm on my way," she calls.

I have to pretend to ring some stuff up at the register so I can collect myself before I face the bar. There's not much to do, but I can't think of anything but Renee and her soft lips and the way she tastes.

Chapter 10

Renee

My aunt lives a town over, in the same town where my mom and her family grew up. Her house is a lot like the house they lived in back then... it hasn't been updated much at all. In this town, most of the houses were built around the same time, by the same company. My aunt's is a one-story with a front porch and a brick walkway and is on a street with ten other houses that look the same. The only difference between the houses is some people chose concrete walkways, and some people chose different shutters for the front window. Some in blue and others in gray.

There are so many memories I have of this place. Back when I was small and my grandpop was alive there were happy times, but then he died and everything changed.

I park by the curb after the drive and take a few deep breaths. It's only when I go to turn the ignition off that I realize I never even turned on the radio. I stare at the windows covered by blinds and prepare myself for what's to come. My aunt's house may be old, but she's kept it up well over the years. It's just her, and she says she doesn't need much. She loves the house and the memories it holds. I love her so darn much and I wish I got to see her more. I wish I got to see her on other occasions.

The snow from last night is already starting to melt in patches in the front yard. She has a corner lot with a tree in the front and the side of the house. In the summertime she'll have plenty of shade and in the fall plenty of leaves to rake up, and the house will look like it's out of a movie about small towns.

With a steadying breath I get out of the car, letting the door shut with a loud thud, and go up to the door and knock softly. My car keys jingle as I toss them in my purse and then brush my hair back from my face. I don't have to wait for anybody to answer. I open the door and step inside; they know I'm coming. It smells clean and cozy like the vanilla candles she likes to burn while she has her morning coffee. For a small moment, I'm hit with nostalgia, the good kind. But the moment doesn't last long at all.

"Hi, I'm here," I call into the house.

"We're just in here, Renee," my aunt answers. Her voice comes from the living room that's through a doorway to the left of the entryway. I take off my boots, hang up my coat on the iron hook that looks like a branch with a bird sitting on top, and pad into the living room. The hardwood floors creak under my weight.

"Hey, Mom." She's on the couch with my aunt, with my aunt's arms around her, and she has a black eye. Emotions choke me for a moment as my mom looks back at me. Her eyes are filled with a look I've seen before. Defeat, betrayal, sadness, but most of all like she's sorry I have to see it.

As tears prick my eyes like I knew they would, I lean down to give both of them a hug. My aunt pretends not to see how emotional I get and tells me she's happy to see me. My mom wraps her arm around my waist and hugs me back while my aunt does the same.

After a long hug, I pat them both on the back and straighten up. "Should I get us some coffee? Tea?"

My aunt wants coffee and my mom wants tea, so I head into the kitchen. I know my way around just fine. It isn't the first time and I'd be naive to think it'll be the last. The kitchen is small and a little dated, but it's squeaky clean and well-organized. I find tea bags above the stove and put water on to boil. A pot of coffee that seems pretty fresh is waiting on the burner of my aunt's coffee machine.

Over the clacking of mugs in the cupboard, I can hear their voices talking quietly while I wait for the water to boil and pour it over the tea bag. I try not to eavesdrop, even though I know my mother will tell me if I ask. She doesn't keep it from me anymore. She hasn't for years. As I try to count how many times we've been in this very situation over the last twelve years, I steep the tea and add a little milk and sugar. Just how she likes it. Then I pour my aunt's coffee, also with a splash of milk. Just how she likes it.

I can›t decide between coffee and tea and finally settle on tea. While it steeps, I bring my mom and aunt their drinks. They›re still sitting close together on the couch, and my mom is wiping at her eyes.

My throat gets tight with frustration, and I go to get my own tea. By the time I get back to the living room and settle into the chair across from them, my mom's eyes are dry again. I can tell it's not the end of her tears, though. She has a dimple in her chin and the corner of her mouth keeps wavering up and down.

I hate him. I hate my father more than he'll ever

know. More than I could ever express. I hate even more that she loves him. Love is for fools.

My mom alternates between deep breaths and sips of her tea.

"I'm really doing it this time." She tries to sound confident but her voice hitches in the middle of her sentence. "I am," she says, and nods like she wants me to nod along with her. I've heard it so many times before though and I used to believe it. Now I just prepare for the next time because there's no hope left.

My aunt rubs at my mom's shoulder, careful not to jostle either of their drinks. "You can stay here as long as you want. You know that, right? You and Renee both know that?"

"Thank you, Aunt Laura," I tell her when she looks at me.

"Neither of you have room for me," my mom says. "I'm not going to be in your way for any longer than I have to."

"You're not in anybody's way," I say, sharing a quick look at my aunt. "You could stay with me. I don't have a spare bedroom but the couch pulls out, and you wouldn't be in my way." She's done it before and I think my place being small and her feeling guilty is what led her to go back. I'm grateful my aunt loves my mom. I'm grateful she can crash here. I just know she doesn't have money and he has it all. I don't have to ask to know he's turned off her cards, probably telling the bank someone stole them. I'm sure the savings and checking accounts are empty. I'm sure she's screwed financially.

He says things will change every single time and they don't. It always ends up like this. My gaze lands on her black eye. Well it hasn't always been *this* bad. Each time it gets a little bit worse.

My aunt waves me off. "Oh, stop it. Renee's place is small. I have the room, and I mean it when I say you can stay here as long as you want. We can be the crazy old ladies who live in the corner house. I have a spare witch's hat you can wear when we pass out candy on Halloween." That gets a small laugh from each of us even though my aunt wears a sad smile.

"If you have a hat, then I guess I can stay," my mom says while wiping the corners of her eyes. She loves my father. She believes him every single time and tells me how it didn't used to be like this. That he's going to change back into the man he was...

My aunt hugs her a little tighter, and they both laugh together, but my mom's face falls as they laugh and tears spill out of her eyes. It's then that I can't help myself and the tears I've been holding back fall too.

We spend the afternoon together and while we do my phone pings. I checked it thinking it was Mags asking me if everything was all right. I didn't tell her every detail, but Mags knows how this goes. Mags did send a message just telling me that she loves me and letting me know she's there if I need anything. But I also got a message from Griffin.

Griffin: *Wish I had the day off with you today. What are you doing?*

I stare at the text knowing damn well he's too kind for me. Too sweet and completely unprepared for the fucked-upness of my life. I don't have the energy to answer, and I don't know what to say so I don't say anything at all. In the back of my mind I know he deserves an answer, but I told him, it's all pretend with him. And right now, my reality is sending me on a spiral I've been on before too many times. I'm not taking him down with me.

After a while my mom excuses herself to the spare bedroom to lie down and apologizes too many times as she does. My aunt and I move quietly into the kitchen. She pulls out the box of tea bags and sighs as the cupboard door closes shut.

"I've been drinking too much coffee. Want another cup of tea?"

"I'd love one," I answer solemnly.

I watch her move about the kitchen in a baggy sweatshirt that might be older than me and a pair of plaid pajama pants. She's always been the caretaker of the family and when I went no contact with my father, she supported me in that decision even when it killed my mother. I know Mom's racked with guilt and just wants it all to be better, but I can't talk to him, think about him, or see him. I want nothing to do with him and Aunt Laura agrees.

With my mug in my hands, I sit at the round kitchen table and straighten the small round tablecloth that my aunt keeps under her sugar dish. It's white with white lace around the outside, and when the spring comes she'll switch it out for one that's green and yellow. She has a matching dish cloth that goes on the oven handle.

It's the tablecloth that suddenly makes me want to cry. My mom does some of the same things as her sister, but it feels like her life is constantly being disrupted by the ever-changing mood of her husband. It seems like a trap she can never get out of no matter how hard she tries.

I'm angry about all the things she can't have, all the things I want her to have. I can picture my mom being happy here for a few years or a couple decades. I can picture her and my aunt cooking dinner together and laughing about their days. As sisters, they've always been close. I don't know what it's like to have a sister, but if I did, I'd want to have a relationship like theirs.

When my mom went back the last time, my aunt had to come to my rescue too. I couldn't believe it. How could she go back to him when he treats her that way?

My aunt says she understands, and we should just be there for her. But I don't. I don't know how you can love someone more than you love yourself. Well I know how but I also know what it does to you, and my mother knows that even better than anyone else.

I can't help but think that I played a part. I'm a big reason that my mom's in this situation in the first place, he even used my name last time. *Come back to me so we can be a real family for Renee*, my father said. I heard him say my name on the phone. I heard him myself and I saw how my mother's expression fell. That's when I decided he could never be in my life again. I thought in that moment my mother agreed. I thought she could see the manipulation as easily as I could.

I was so wrong.

My aunt pours water over the tea bags in two mugs, then leans on the countertop and looks at me, her expression patient.

"Do you think she'll really leave him this time?" I ask, keeping my voice quiet so I don't wake my mom...and so she doesn't overhear. This isn't a question I can ask my mom today, or maybe ever. The only way I could even see her again after she went back the last time was if she promised to never mention him to me again.

My aunt purses her lips. "I hope so. Have you spoken to him?"

I shake my head, looking out the kitchen window to my aunt's tidy backyard. There's a white fence between her yard and her neighbor to the back. The fence is low enough that you could stand on either side and chat. My aunt has flower baskets that she puts at the base of her fence in the areas where her garden doesn't reach. It's a nice place to sit and have a cup of tea when the weather's nice.

That's what my mom could be doing this summer if she left for good and let my aunt take care of her for a while. Not forever, if that's not what she wants, but for long enough that she can figure out how she feels about everything and what she wants to do with her life.

"I haven't," I tell her. "I blocked him the last time this happened. I haven't spoken to him in almost a year."

She knows this. But maybe she thought I was more like my mother. That I wouldn't be able to let him go. He's never hurt me physically. Only yelled at me and berated me growing up. He kept me in line with fear. Now I stay far away from him. I know the man he truly is.

"I want nothing to do with him ever again," I tell her.

My aunt nods, her eyes compassionate. "Are you

doing okay, baby?"

I nod back, my throat even tighter now. "I'm doing all right."

I really mean it—I'm doing all right. I have my job at the bar and my apartment and whatever this thing is with Griffin. I can't even think about him right now. I'm so ashamed. How could a person like him even fathom what having parents like mine is like. I'm reminded of Christmas and how I told him we usually don't do anything. I lied. My mother texted me and begged me to forgive my father on Christmas Eve. The only thing she wanted was for us to be a family again. The only thing I did on Christmas was cry alone in my apartment until my mother came over and said she was sorry and that she loved me, and we stayed up watching Christmas movies and pretended like the day before never happened.

I don't know what this Christmas will be like. I don't know if she'll be here or back with her husband. I don't know anything other than that Griffin offered me an escape. I shouldn't have taken it, but I couldn't say no to that...just in case.

My emotions must show more than I think because my aunt makes a sound I know all too well. That pitiful one she gives to my mother.

"Oh, honey." My aunt crosses the kitchen, pulls me to my feet, and gives me a tight hug. I rest my head on her shoulder and breathe slow and deep so I don't keep crying. I really don't want to spend my whole visit in tears. I'm not the one with the black eye, and I know crying about it won't help.

It takes me a few minutes to stop. My aunt grabs me some tissues from the box on the counter, then goes to finish the tea while I put myself back together. She brings both mugs to the kitchen table and we sit around the curve from one another with our tea. I hold the warm mug in my palms before taking a sip, letting the warmth steady me.

"Renee," my aunt says. She's a lot like Mags. She can always tell when something's on my mind. It's not in my head, really, it's in my chest. The feeling of guilt is so heavy at times like these that it's hard to take a deep breath. I do it anyway and drink some more of my tea. It tastes better than when I made it, though it's the same kind.

"Yeah?" I say, when I feel like I can speak again.

"It's really no trouble at all to have your mom stay with me. I'm happy to have her here, even if that means having her here for the rest of our lives. You don't have to worry about me... or her."

"I know," I tell her. "I know you're okay with it."

I really do. My aunt doesn't want my mom with him, and she's an honest person. She's not lying about wanting my mom to stay with her. I honestly think it would be the perfect situation.

I look at her, and there's nothing but concern in my aunt's face. The pressure on my chest feels even heavier. If I leave without saying anything, it'll be there until the next time I visit. It'll probably be there for the rest of my life. I don't see the way I feel changing.

I just wish it would. I wish I could have everything together, including my mom in a place that's good for her, and I wish I could wake up every day without all this painful guilt.

"She would have left him in the beginning if it wasn't for me." My aunt's eyebrows go up a little at my words. "You and I both know that."

My aunt reaches across the table and takes my hand in hers. Her fingers are warm from the mug of tea, and she gives my hand a gentle squeeze. "Renee, you know this isn't your fault, right?"

I don't answer her. Cause the first time she left him I begged her to go back home. I was a kid. I didn't know any better and I told her it was true love. It is my fault. At least a piece of it. And I'll never forgive myself. I'll never believe in true love again.

CHAPTER 11

GRIFFIN

When I pull up to the entrance of the drive-in movie, the sign has the title of the movie and the genre in all caps below it. HORROR, it says.

I look at Renee with a serious expression. She's sitting in the passenger seat of my car, leaning forward a few inches to read the title of the movie. There are pillows and blankets in the back along with popcorn from the gas station and boxes of chocolate covered peanuts that she told me a while ago were her favorites.

"Oooh, a scary one?" Renee asks, her eyebrows raised. She looks beautiful tonight. Red is her color. Her coat is already off and thrown in the back seat, and her dark red sweater dress nearly matches the color of her lips. "Horror for our first fake date," she says comically.

"Are you brave enough for it?" I say back and then add, "It was our only option, unfortunately." We were supposed to go out yesterday but something came up for her. On Sundays there's only one movie that plays so... here we are. I'm happy with it though, if she is.

Her smile falters, and she looks down at the center console. "I'm brave enough for anything," she says, but she doesn't sound like she believes it. Or like her mind went elsewhere.

I want to ask her if everything's okay, but I bite my tongue because I've already asked once. She was so quiet on the drive over, and the tone of her voice makes me think there's something going on. It's like that day in the bar when she came in looking sad, and I want to know what it is so I can fix it.

My hands twist on the steering wheel and I stay quiet. I have the feeling Renee would think that wasn't a pretend-date thing to talk about, though, and trying to start that conversation might push her away. Then we'd be back to one-word answers over text.

When I glance back over at her, she's smiling and I'll take that. The last thing I want is to mess this up with her. So I drive ahead with a forced smile and pray this movie is good, or if it isn't, we can cuddle up and get these windows to fog.

There are ten or so other cars at the movie tonight. I pull into the lot and find a spot that has a decent view of the screen without being too close to anybody else. We don't need them looking in the windows on our "pretend date." In this spot, we're mostly behind the other cars, too, so nobody will see us, really.

Renee rolls down her window just enough to position the speaker and when she's done, she glances over at me.

I give her a serious look. "I have to ask you something."

"What?" she asks, obviously worried. My heart squeezes. I'm just trying to lighten the mood and make her feel less down, and I'm screwing it up already.

"Do you like to have a huge bucket of popcorn at the drive-in? You can say no, but I didn't want to assume you were a popcorn person and make an ass of myself."

Renee laughs, and that makes my heart feel a hell of a lot lighter. Her eyes crinkle and she covers her mouth, then drops her hand back to her lap.

"I *am* a popcorn person, actually," she says. "What about you?"

"I feel like it should be illegal not to have popcorn at the drive-in."

"With extra butter?" she asks.

"Always," I say with more seriousness that forces

her to laugh. That's better. That sweet sound eases the tension.

"Let me grab the bag from the back." I hustle to the trunk and immediately check the two bags of popcorn. It's unreal that I should feel this much relief that one of the bags says "extra butter," but then again being with this woman does something to me and she knows it.

In the other car windows I can see some people›s faces in the light of their phones, and they›re all busy, talking or texting and just passing the time until the movie starts.

As I close the trunk and head back to the driver seat, the screen lights up with directions for how to put the speakers on the car window.

"Come on!" Renee calls, waving her hand at me to hurry me up and reaching for the bags in my arms. "You're going to miss the previews."

"Don't worry, I'm not missing the previews." I hand over the bottles of water and drinks and the popcorn, then put the rest on the center console and slide into my seat. "See? They haven't even—"

That's exactly when the previews start, and the volume on our speaker is turned up high.

"Woah!" Renee grabs for the speaker and finds the volume knob, turning it down quickly, then readjusting it back up. Her cheeks turn pink in the light from the movie, and she gives me a nervous smile. "Sorry about that. Maybe I'm not cut out for drive-in movies."

"No harm done." The preview on the screen is gory. "Can't say the same for this preview."

Renee makes a face and looks down at the popcorn, opening the bag with extra butter. She picks out a few pieces and eats them. I've never seen someone eat popcorn in a sexy way, but Renee pulls it off. I could watch her eat popcorn all night. "This is *really* good popcorn."

"I got these too." I hand her the chocolates and she smiles so wide it reaches her eyes. "Those are the right ones, right?" I ask and she looks at me for a moment, really looking at me before nodding, saying "yeah," and smiling like I just made her night.

We settle in with the blankets and pillows, leaning back as the previews play. I jump back at a cheap shock value moment, and she laughs.

"That's embarrassing," I tell her and laugh along with her. Time passes easily and I love how she's more relaxed than she was on the drive. Whatever it is that she was thinking about doesn't seem like it's on her mind anymore.

She glances at me, then the screen again her expression flinching. "The one we're seeing isn't this bloody, is it?"

"I think it said it was more of a thriller but with horror elements," I tell her. I looked up the movie before we came to make sure it wasn't one of those slasher ones. Didn't seem like good pretend-date material.

"Good." Renee takes a second to hit the door locks.

"If it's really scary, I'll protect you. I'm not afraid to drive away with the speaker still attached in an emergency." She laughs and playfully nudges me before going back to the chocolates and popcorn.

We get quiet and watch the rest of the previews, and I start to think this is going to be a date to brag about to Brody.

Then the movie starts and the screen goes dark at the very beginning. Renee's in shadow but she's still the most beautiful person I've ever seen. I try to look at her out of the corner of my eye, but I end up turning my head just to drink her in. She catches me looking when the scene on the screen turns to afternoon in somebody's front yard and grins at me.

"You going to stare at me the whole movie?" I whisper, like we're in a theater full of people instead of my car at the drive-in.

"You were the one staring," she whispers back, and eats some more popcorn. "Are you scared of the movie already?"

"I'm not scared of anything," I tell her, and look

back at the screen. It's not true. I *am* scared of some things, like having this whole pretend-date thing go south or scaring her off before she can be my fake date for Christmas. I'm scared that something's on her mind that's too big for one person to deal with, but she's not telling me because I'm her boss.

Clearing my throat, I settle into the seat and grab my drink.

I push all that to the back of my mind and try to concentrate on the movie. It's tough because Renee smells amazing. I've got the heat going in the car to keep us warm, so it's blowing the scent of her into my face every second.

Renee's totally into the movie, though, her eyes wide and her hand moving slowly through the popcorn. She likes the buttery pieces and eats them one at a time, savoring each one. It's the cutest thing I've ever seen.

I wait until there's a montage on the screen to lean over, just like I would in a real theater.

"Hey."

Renee leans toward me, our arms brushing against each other on the center console. "Hey," she says, her voice low.

"Wanted to tell you something, if now's a good time," I say, matching her volume.

"Before they get back to finding the murderer,"

Renee says.

"Okay." There's a short phone call on the screen. "I, uh, I like kissing you."

Renee snorts, then starts laughing. She laughs even harder through the next scene, when the hero and heroine are trying to find the city's scariest killer, now with the extra information they got from the house where the last murder had taken place.

"How do you *do* that?" she asks, her voice shaky like she might start laughing again.

I can't take my eyes off her.

"Do what?" I ask, my voice low.

Renee takes a breath, then turns and finds me watching. Her eyes move slowly over my face, down to my lips and back up again. Her breath catches.

"Make me feel like..." Her eyes stay on my face for a few beats more. In the light from the drive-in screen, I can see Renee's face flushing a deeper red. She glances away, biting her lip. "I don't know."

I shuffle myself toward the screen and pretend to watch the movie. I'm actually looking at her, just in my peripheral vision. Her arm presses against mine on the center console.

"Like what?" I ask.

She's quiet for long enough that I have to look over at her without hiding it. Renee's eyes meet mine, and she shakes her head. The tension between us is thick. It doesn't even matter that she's holding a bag of popcorn that's two-thirds full. I wouldn't care if the whole thing tipped over and got everywhere. That's how much I want her in my arms.

Slowly, holding my breath, I move my arm against hers.

Renee doesn't pull away. Her breath gets a little quicker and shallower. I get another breath of her scent and it takes effort not to stroke her hair back from her face.

Instead I take her hand in mine. My hand is bigger than hers, but when I thread our fingers together, they fit perfectly.

Renee looks down our hands, then back up into my eyes.

"Do you want to come to my place after?" I ask.

She lets out a breath like she's been waiting for me to ask her that question all night. Damn—did I screw up again? Should I have asked her before we drove all the way here?

I decide it doesn't matter because Renee looks at me and nods.

"Yeah," she says, and sits up, giving me a kiss on the cheek, all the while holding that bag of popcorn steady without moving her hand from mine. "I do."

CHAPTER 12

RENEE

Griffin holds my hand all the way to his house, running soothing circles over my knuckles with the pad of his thumb. It's not too far from my apartment in a little neighborhood that reminds me of my aunt's. By the time we get there, I'm not thinking about my aunt at all. I'm not thinking about anything but how strong his hand feels around mine. I wanted him so much when we were at the drive-in; I want him to take me away from reality and we can get lost together, tangled in sheets this time instead of the bar.

I just want to forget and pretend with him.

He gets out of the car and jogs around to the passenger side. It makes me laugh. He doesn't have to do that. He's too damn nice. Griffin smiles when he opens the door for me, and I can't help but to smile back. He takes my hand in his and helps me out, and then we're both in a cold breeze that feels even colder now that it's dark out.

The butterflies in the pit of my stomach flutter like crazy as he walks beside me and hustles me in and out of the cold. I feel like I'm getting away with something on the way to his front door. He pulls out a key, unlocks the door, and pulls me inside. I can't stop looking at him. His five o'clock shadow is handsome and looks perfect on his sharp jaw.

His entryway is neat and small, and that's all I see of it before he pushes me back against the door and kisses me. My coat is half way off and he helps me the rest of the way as I moan and suck his bottom lip. He smiles against my lips and then kisses me again, deeper this time.

"Renee," he groans my name, in a low sexy voice. I love it. I'm lost in the way he craves me.

I push at his coat first and then his button down. His hands move up my sweater dress and our clothes fall to the floor in a puddle beneath us. All the while my breath quickens, and I can't stop kissing him. He can't stop kissing me either.

Griffin's hands slide around my waist and in a swift motion that makes me gasp, he picks me up off the floor. Feeling his smile at my lips, I wrap my legs around his hips and get comfortable in his embrace. Griffin holds me close against him, and I love the sexy groan he makes before he kisses me again.

It's a relief to be in a house away from everyone's prying eyes. I hesitate for a second, because I'm not used to that—the only times we've touched or kissed have been at the bar, where someone could've tried to walk in or looked through the window. Now I'm sure there's nobody watching. It's freeing in so many ways.

I spear my fingers into his hair and Griffin tips his face up toward mine. He never stops kissing me as he braces my back against the foyer wall.

"Your house is nice," I tell him in between kisses as the butterflies in my stomach move lower and lower. "Want to show me the rest of it?"

Griffin laughs. "How 'bout I show you my bedroom?"

He carries me through the first room and I don't notice a damn thing other than how the cords in his arms make them feel even more muscular. And how broad his shoulders are as my fingers slip down them, and I kiss down his neck.

"Living room," he says, nodding his head toward one doorway. "Kitchen's back there. I have a gym down in the basement, but we don't have to look at that right now." He carries me up a flight of stairs. "Bathroom," he says, nodding his head again. "And here's the best part."

He carries me through another doorway to his bedroom, which is larger than I thought it would be. Griffin gives me a minute to look around and I try to catch my breath. He keeps it neat, same as the bar. There's a chair with one of his sweatshirts thrown over it and a decent-sized closet. I tip my face down and kiss him again, content on looking around another time. Right now I just want him.

Griffin kisses me back, slower this time but just as deep. He doesn't seem to have any trouble balancing me and he lowers me carefully to the bed.

"I want to take my time with you, my little tease," he murmurs against my chest as his mouth moves lower, his hands at the waistband of my leggings. "Can I?" Goosebumps spread along my skin and my gaze follows down my body, watching his eyes roam my curves and then lower.

"All the time you want," I say. Lust fills my head at the feeling of him tugging my pants over my hips. All I can hear is our heavy breathing. His finger tips are slow and deliberate and send shivers of want down my body. Griffin undresses me slowly and carefully, tossing my clothes over to the chair with his sweatshirt.

My heart races and heat flows through my body as he caresses between my legs. His deft fingers massage over my clit and my head falls back against the pillows, the heels of my feet digging into the bed as the warmth and pleasure force small moans from me.

A deep groan of pleasure comes from his chest, which brings my gaze to his, and I nearly come undone at the sight of him, toying with me before he lowers his lips to my clit and sucks.

"Griffin," I moan his name and my blunt nails dig into his sheets as I chase the high of release and find it crashing around me all at once.

As I fall back from my release, he leans over me on the bed, staring at me with his lips slightly parted and his eyes dark. He hasn't turned on any of the lights in his bedroom; there's only the moonlight slipping through the windows. It's plenty enough to see him.

Our eyes meet. My hands move from his shoulders to his hair. I can't stop touching him. I need him. I need Griffin more than I need air to breathe right now.

"I need you," I murmur and the man smirks down at me. "I know you do," he says and the blush I'm so damn used to with him floods into my cheeks.

He stays leaning over me while he strips off his shirt and undershirt and then pushes down his boxers. When he crawls onto the bed with me, sliding us both up toward the pillows, he's finally naked.

"You're so hot," I breathe and for a split moment, with the chill of the air against my heated face, I remember we're on a date.

A pretend date.

Griffin's body against mine is anything but pretend. He lowers his head to my collarbone and kisses me there, one of his hands running up and down my side.

He moves to tease me again, kissing down my body. He licks and nips my heated skin like we have all night, his tongue curving over all the most sensitive places before he moves up and concentrates on my clit.

With the tortuous need overwhelming me, I practically beg him, "I want you to fuck me."

He groans in response and leaves an open-mouthed kiss on my inner thigh. "I want you too," he whispers as his body hovers over mine. I lift my legs to wrap them around his waist. That's when the tip of his cock makes contact with my entrance. A shiver moves over my body from head to toe.

In a swift motion he pushes inside me. I let out a moan into the crook of his neck as the pleasure runs through me, every nerve ending lighting with a roaring flame. I hook my feet behind his back, pulling him in faster, urging him for more and more. He takes it slow, though, filling me and making the pleasure so much deeper.

He holds himself over me, not putting too much weight on me while he presses himself against me. I hook my arms around his neck and pull him down into a kiss. It takes my breath away to feel him everywhere like this, even inside me, while he explores me with his tongue and his lips and moans into my mouth.

"Fuck, Renee," he says, his breath heating up my neck. He turns his head and drags his mouth over the same spot. "This is all I've ever wanted."

My heart beats even faster. I push myself back against him, arching my back to get the most contact I possibly can. This is all I've ever wanted, too, even before I knew I wanted it. I've never felt so much pleasure tingling down to my fingertips and my toes. I think it can't get any better until Griffin slides his hand down my waist and finds my clit with his fingertips.

I get lost in the heat and pleasure, throwing my head back and letting out every feeling in moans that I couldn't stop if I wanted to.

Griffin kisses my neck. "That's it, you dirty little tease. I want to feel you come. I need this so fucking bad."

My orgasm grows until I'm moving against his fingers and against his cock, and then it reaches a peak.

I don't feel anything but him all the way through my orgasm. My entire body trembles as I crash into the waves of my release. Griffin holds me tighter against him, his hips moving faster, chasing his own climax just after mine. He pulses inside of me and all the while his lips brush against the crook of my neck. My heartbeat slowly falls as I take account of just how fucking intense it all was.

When he's done, he turns me over, cleans us up and lays me on the pillows, then lies down next to me and kisses my jaw. I turn my head and kiss him back. I think he might catch his breath after a second and maybe lie down to rest, but the longer I kiss him, the longer he kisses me back. Until sleep finds us both.

CHAPTER 13

GRIFFIN

The morning comes too soon, and I wake up thinking it's all been a hell of a dream.

When I open my eyes enough to see that Renee is actually in my bed, cuddled up against me and fast asleep, a smile stretches across my face. I'm careful not to move too much and disturb her.

Holy shit.

She's fucking beautiful too. Sleeping soundly, her chest rises and falls with every peaceful breath. I close my eyes again and let myself float in the memories from last night. Renee practically jumped on me when we got inside. My cock hardens as I remember her hands on me, tugging at my clothes, and going after exactly what she wanted.

Her entire body was telling me how much she wanted me, from her slim hips to her thighs wrapping around my waist to the way she lifted herself up to get my lips on more of her.

Damn, last night was fucking good.

Renee doesn't seem anywhere close to waking up, so I get out of bed as slowly and carefully as I can and take a few seconds to look at her.

The sun's just coming up, and Renee looks beautiful in the early morning light. Her auburn hair is a messy halo all over my pillow and her lips are just slightly parted while she dreams.

I tiptoe into my closet and throw on sweatpants and a sweatshirt, then go quietly into the bathroom to wash my face and brush my teeth. Neither of us is scheduled to be at the bar until later, so there's no rush to wake her up.

The first thing I do when I get downstairs is tidy up. I pick up our coats and Renee's purse from the floor.

When everything's in its place, I go to the kitchen. A burst of air comes out of the fridge when I open it, and I shiver at the cold.

Pancakes. I'll make Renee pancakes.

My mom taught me how to make good pancakes

years ago, so I take the milk out of the fridge and go to get a bowl and pancake mix. There are a few other ingredients if you want them to taste amazing, so I get some sugar and vanilla extract and put those out on the counter, too. It reminds me of home to put the mix into the bowl and add milk, stirring until it's at the right consistency and then adding the eggs.

Once I've done that, I go and hunt down my phone. I left it in my coat pocket last night. I don't think I've done that in years. It's a bit reckless in case something happens with Brody or the bar or my family, and I'm relieved to pick it up and see that nobody called.

I text Brody on the way to the kitchen.

Griffin: *You awake?*

My phone goes off with a short buzz of vibration on the counter just as I get back to the pancake mix.

Brody: *Yeah? Everything okay?*

Griffin: *More than okay*

I finish putting together the pancake mix so I don't add anything twice, then get out a pan and put it on the stove to heat.

Brody: *Was last night movie night?*

Griffin: *It ended up being more than movie night. She stayed at my place*

Pride fills my chest as I pour some of the batter into the pan, grinning like a fool. By the time I pick up my phone again, there are three new messages from Brody.

Brody: *Holy shit, dude*

Brody: *You move quick*

Brody: *Did you even stay until the end of the movie?*

I stifle a laugh, doing my best to keep it quiet so I don't wake Renee. I don't know what time she normally gets up, but at my place, she can sleep as long as she wants.

Brody: *Congratulations, man. I knew it would work out with you and Renee*

His message makes me pause. Staying at my place overnight is a step in the right direction, but I don't know if it's a sign that things are smooth sailing forever. She might even joke that it's still a pretend date, knowing how she's been so far.

Griffin: *I'm hoping it works out in the long run*

Griffin: *I really, really like her*

Brody: *I can tell. She likes you too*

I flip the pancakes in the pan, then pick up my phone again.

Griffin: *You and Mags doing okay?*

Brody: *Yeah, pretty much. She's focused on the baby room and getting everything in there*

Griffin: *Anything you guys need? Anything I can bring for you?*

I pour some more batter into the pan after piling up the first pancakes.

Brody: *We're just lying low this morning, waiting for her to pop, everything's good*

I huff a laugh at that before responding.

Griffin: *You tell me if you need anything, okay?*

Brody: *I will, thanks man*

With that I leave him alone. I know he's got a lot on his mind. They already have Bridget, but this experience is different for him. I expect when the little one arrives I'll see him less often but at the same time, I can't wait for him to be holding that baby. I'm happy he got his happily ever after and then some.

I flip the last few pancakes and arrange them onto two plates, butter them, and then heat up some syrup in a mug before pouring into the middle of each stack. I find two cloth napkins that my mom gave me as a housewarming gift when I moved in and wrap them around a knife and fork for each of us. I've never used them before, but it seems like something that might impress Renee.

Knowing Renee will want coffee, I find the grounds and start a pot brewing, thinking I can come back down for it after I give her the pancakes, still hot and fresh.

And then I climb the stairs, trying not to smile too hard. I make it up to my bedroom without spilling the plates and nudge the door open with my elbow.

Renee's standing at the foot of the bed, pulling her

shirt on over her head. She sees me when her head pops through the neck, and her eyes go wide.

"Good morning," she says in a rush, her face going red.

My heart sinks fast but I try not to show it. "I didn't know you were up. Are you all right?"

"I'm fine. I'm good," Renee says, running her fingers through her hair and shaking it out. "I just have to head out."

"Oh." *Fuck.* "Where are you going?"

"I just—" Renee looks around and bites her lip, obviously worried. Out of all of the possibilities this morning, I didn't anticipate this. I struggle for a moment not knowing exactly what to say.

"If you're looking for your purse, it's downstairs."

"I was," Renee admits and then glances down to the breakfast in my hands. "I'm really sorry you made breakfast."

"Don't worry about it." I put the plates down on my dresser and pull myself back together. "You need a ride to your place, don't you? I'll take you there right now. Unless you need to be somewhere else."

"I have an appointment." Renee looks away from me with a frown on her face and a look in her eyes that looks like guilt. "I can always call Mags for a ride, if you don't want—"

"Don't do that. I want to take you." Something awful

settles in my chest as I stare at Renee, wondering what the hell is going on. I almost ask her again if she's sure she's okay, but I already know she'll tell me she is when she obviously isn't. All I can think is to not push her, that she'll tell me.

"Are you sure?" She looks up at me, obviously worried about something and the question is right there on the tip of my tongue. "I should have told you last night I had to leave early," she says softly and then brushes her hair back from her face. "I feel like a jerk, now that you made breakfast." She offers a sad smile in apology, and I can't stand her thinking that pancakes are worth getting upset over.

I shrug, it's fine. "Forget about breakfast," I tell her softly. "There'll be another chance to have breakfast." I hope so, anyway. "Let me get you home."

Chapter 14

Renee

The divorce lawyer's office is in the town where my mom used to live. She has a small, swanky looking office on the main street. When I get there, my mom is seated in the waiting area out front with tears in her eyes, looking down at her phone. Her black jeans look a bit loose as does her sweater. I imagine they're my aunt's. But her hair is done and so is her makeup. The foundation is doing a piss poor job of covering that bruise around her eye.

The sight of her like this will keep me up at night. It breaks my heart. And the guilt of sleeping in and being late takes over with every step closer I get.

She looks up at me when she hears my shoes clacking against the stone floor and stands up to hug me. It's a firm hug and she rests her shoulder a moment longer than normal. "Renee," she says in a small voice against my shoulder.

"Hi, Mom. You okay?" I ask her and she looks me up and down. I'm still in the clothes from last night. No time to change but I think it looks okay. Or at least I thought it did.

"You look beautiful, baby girl," she says. Baby girl is her nickname for me, and it makes me smile.

"I'm sorry you had to come all the way out here, especially in this traffic," she says.

"It's not a long drive," I lie, because I don't want her to feel any worse than she already does. I got her text when Griffin was downstairs making breakfast. She's really going to do it. She's going to leave him for good. She said she took the first appointment available. There was a cancellation, and she was going. She's really going to do it. "You need someone with you," I tell her and grab her hand.

I almost didn't reply when she first messaged. Then guilt got the better of me. When she said she's here and was scared but ready, I asked her if Aunt Laura was with her. She isn't.

I don't want my mom to be alone for this. I also don't want her to back out because she's scared. It doesn't ease the guilt I felt when Griffin came up the stairs with pancakes. Someday I'm going to have a life that doesn't feel like this, I promise myself. "You don't have to worry about me, okay?" I tell my mom.

"I do." My mom takes my hand and pulls me into the seat next to her. The sofa in the lawyer's office looks nice, but it's too hard to be truly comfortable. It's nothing like Griffin's bed. I woke up so warm and comfortable and satisfied this morning that I wanted to roll over and go back to sleep, but then I heard sounds in the kitchen and realized he was making breakfast, and I didn't want to be a mess...then the texts came. It took everything not to get emotional while alone in his bedroom. I'm proud I at least kept it together until I got to my car.

My mom squeezes my hand. "I do worry about you."

I don't know what to say to that, but I offer up, "Mom, it's okay."

She shakes her head, new tears shine in her eyes. "I thought I was doing the right thing by you, Renee. I hope you know that you were always on my mind and I'm so sorry I couldn't see right or think right or—" Her words become breathless and rushed and I cut her off.

"I know you did." I could see that in my mom's face every time she went back to him. It took me a long time to see everything for what it was. I almost tell her, but the words don't come. "I just love you," I tell her, settling on that and squeezing her hand tight.

"I love you baby girl," my mother says and wipes under her eyes. "One of these days I'll stop crying and be there for you like I should."

She still had hope that it would all work out, and that this time he'd change for the better, and my throat closes up with how guilty I feel about that. Maybe she wouldn't have tried to look for the positives if it wasn't for me. Maybe, if she'd been by herself without me to think of, she'd have looked for a better life for herself. All the what ifs pile up in the back of my head and I do everything I can to shut them all down. "Seriously, Mom, don't think about that right now. I'm okay."

"I loved him." She presses her lips into a thin line and looks out the window of the lawyer's office. There's a fancy coffee machine with a stack of coffee pods arranged in a pyramid next to it. Somehow the arrangement seems almost like a promise, like the lawyer can fight her way into the kind of life where you have enough money for a coffee machine that costs eight hundred dollars and an endless stack of pods in the shape of a pyramid. And you never get a black eye from a man who's supposed to love you. "I really loved him."

"I get it," I whisper, then clear my throat and say it

again, loud enough for her to hear me this time. "I get it. But that's not what love is." I loved him too. I remember loving him and feeling like he loved me back. Those moments hurt the most. It's like a death. That's what my therapist said. It's mourning. And every time she went back to him, I mourned the loss of that love all over again.

My mom parts her lips, and I don't know what she's going to say but it seems important. But before she can, a woman who looks about my age in a pencil skirt and a simple but chic blazer comes out into the waiting area.

"Ms. Blair?" she says, crossing the room toward us and offering us both her hand. We both stand up.

"Yes, and this is my daughter, Renee." My mother's left hand lands on my shoulder and she stands a little taller.

We both shake the woman's hand. "I'm Janet, Ms. Cane's assistant," she says. "Let me take you back to her office. Can I get you anything to drink? Tea? Water? Coffee?"

"I'd love a coffee please," I say. I need the caffeine immediately.

"A tea would be wonderful," my mom answers and adds, "thank you." The assistant nods and steps out of the door as the lawyer comes forward to meet us. A tall woman made even taller with heels. She wears a slimming gray pantsuit and has dark, curly hair, a polite and professional smile, and bright eyes.

"Lindsey," she greets my mother, shaking her hand

with both of hers, one on top and one on bottom. Her warmth is obvious, and I already like her.

"Ms. Cane," my mother greets her back.

"You can call me Donna," she says softly, and I see her gaze move to my mother's black eye, but her expression doesn't falter.

She ushers us to a small meeting table off to the side of her office. My mom and I take two chairs along one side. Ms. Cane takes a chair at the head of the table and spreads a folder open on the table.

"I think we should start with a discussion of your circumstances while the marriage was still intact," she says, looking my mom in the eye. "Did you work outside the home?"

The corner of my mom's mouth turns down. She looks at her hands in her lap, then back up at the lawyer. "No, I didn't. I tried to get a job a couple of times, but it never panned out."

It never panned out because my father didn't want her out of the house. Whenever she would leave, he'd find ways to get her to come back, and then it was her job to put things back together at home. I told her he did it on purpose, but she defended him. She didn't want to see it, or she couldn't admit it. Admitting something like that would have a domino effect. Once one truth is out, they all escape. I know it's hard to face and it's easier to just not believe it. It's so much easier to just make an excuse.

My mom answers more questions about her life with John, my father. I've heard most of it before and all the while I hold her hand. I stay quiet and try to stay steady.

As she talks about different things that have happened, I remember Griffin this morning.

How Griffin was this morning. He let me sleep and went downstairs to make breakfast. He didn't seem upset with me even once on the drive to my place. The last thing he said to me when I got out of the car was *are you sure you don't need a ride to your appointment? I really don't mind driving you*, and when I said no, he said *text me when you're there safe.*

I wonder how long that would last. I wonder if it's genuine. I wonder if once I fall for him, will he change?

Cause I don't know what the switch was exactly, but my father used to act like he loved her. I remember as a child thinking they loved each other and looking up to them.

He used to take care of her. And my mother admits it to the lawyer all the while I have to sit there, wondering what happened. What changed? How did that man I used to love turn into the person he is now? Or was he just really good at hiding from the very beginning?

The last year I was around them I watched him manipulate her and make her promises that were clearly lies, but he never seemed to worry about her, except when he was worried that she wouldn't go along with what he said. The look in Griffin's eyes this morning... I've never seen that from John.

The worst part was how my father would apologize. I never thought he meant it, but he said it so many times that it was easier for my mom to agree with him. And then there were me, the lack of money or a savings account, and how hard it was for her to find work. She always went back, no matter how many times he yelled at her or hit her or how terrible he was. It got progressively worse when I moved out. I didn't realize just how bad it was until two years ago and the moment I said it out loud, all the pieces fell. I couldn't put them back into place. They fell and I saw clearly for the first time. Every little thing I'd noticed before but I'd made excuses for, screamed back at me: I told you so!

My mother continues to answer questions, and her even and strong tone brings me back to the present.

Tears burn my eyes thinking about how much my mom deserves a man who actually cares. I wipe them away as subtly as I can and square my shoulders.

I clear my head and focus back on the conversation. The lawyer is professional and warm, but from the expression on her face, there's not much in my mom's case that's going to make it easy for her.

"I'll be straightforward with you," the lawyer says, closing the folder and folding her hands on top of it. "This is the kind of case that can take years if the other party is determined to drag his feet. It's costly, and without funds to split there are only so many motions we can file in order to help you until settlement."

"Wait, she should have half right now, shouldn't she?" The shock in my tone is undeniable. If he has money to spend, she should also. "He can't just turn off her cards and not pay a consequence for financial abuse." My voice is harsh and as the lawyer looks back at me with what seems like sympathy, I realize I don't know a damn thing about actual legal proceedings.

"We can file motions to freeze accounts and file for an audit; there's a lot we can do," the lawyer says and then corrects herself, "there's a lot we *will* do. There's a way for this, but what I'm saying is that currently I cannot say with certainty how much you are entitled to or what is even available or when this would all end."

My mother is silent, and I reach for her hand as the lawyer continues. "And I'm certainly not suggesting that you disregard what you want out of the settlement. I do want to be clear that because the house is in his name and he can show that he owned the property before you were married, he might be able to make the argument that the house should be considered his property. Were there any other assets you had in your name that you can think of? Any other properties or vehicles?"

Out of the corner of my eye, I can see my mom's shoulders slump, but she straightens up right away.

"I didn't have any vehicles in my name," she says. "He might have other properties, but if he does, I don't know anything about them."

"We can look into it." The lawyer writes something down on a notepad. "It's important to me that you decide on a course of action that's best for you. If your first priority is to dissolve the marriage and start setting up a life that's unconnected to your ex, then that might ultimately mean walking away from discussions about the property."

"Because he'll want to fight," my mom says softly.

"Unfortunately, it's a tactic that's often used in contentious divorces," the lawyer says. There's real sympathy in her eyes. I believe her when she says it's unfortunate. I have to think she's seen situations like my mom's before. "Some people are more interested in punishing the other party than they are in moving on from the case."

Anger swells up in my chest. It's hot and overwhelming. For some reason, it's worse that the lawyer is describing this in such professional terms. I know it's her job to stay calm and distance herself from the emotions of the case so that she can make objective decisions, but I want her to be angrier about this, too.

"She was a stay-at-home mom for years. And she stayed at home because he wanted her to," I press.

"I understand, and I will do everything I can to make sure your mother receives alimony, but it is up to the discretion of the judge," she warns. "And it will take time."

"So she's just screwed until...when?" I ask, defeated and angry. "No money to live on while fighting a man who's going to use the legal system to abuse her more."

"Renee," my mom says, disapproving.

"That's what you mean," I tell the lawyer. "That's what abusers do."

"That's what I mean, yes," the lawyer says. "Though in the context of the case, we won't make much headway trying to frame his behavior that way."

"We don't have to frame it as anything—that's what it was."

Ms. Cane raises a hand. "I completely agree. But in a divorce settlement, the judge won't be looking to award any properties as a penalty for his behavior. The worst-case scenario is that it becomes a situation where both parties spend a significant amount of time trying to get judgment on the events that occurred, not dissolving the marriage. A criminal case would be entirely separate."

I lean back in my chair, the fight going out of me. My

mom has never been willing to press charges. So without that evidence it may go nowhere.

That's essentially what the lawyer is saying right now.

"Okay," I say. "I'm sorry. It upsets me sometimes, thinking about..." I wave my hand and sit up straighter. "I'm fine. Sorry about that."

The discussion goes on for a few more minutes and it boils down to the most likely outcome, which is that my mom walks away from her marriage with nothing, and her ex-husband gets everything.

But she'd be done with him.

We go out into the cold after the meeting, my mom puts her arms around me.

"I'm okay," I say, hugging her back. "And you're going to be okay, too."

"I'm the one who's supposed to be telling you that," she says with a quiet laugh that sounds far too sad. The bitter cold whips across our faces as we head to her car, but I don't get in.

"I have to go home; I have work tonight," I tell her, and she nods in understanding although her expression changes to something I don't understand at first.

"We'll find you a job. Aunt Laura will know some places where you can work that won't take all your energy, and you can start putting money away."

"That's right," my mom says, her voice shaking a

little. "I'm going to figure this out, don't you worry," she tells me, a little more optimistic.

"Yes, you will." I hug her tighter.

"Will you come home for Christmas?" my mom asks without letting go of me. "To your aunt's, I mean?"

I nod against her shoulder. "I'll be there, Mom. I promise."

CHAPTER 15

GRIFFIN

I get one text from Renee midway through the morning and I'm relieved to see her name on my phone. More than relieved.

Renee: *Back home fine. I'll be in for my shift tonight*

She didn't seem upset about whatever appointment she had, but she didn't seem happy about it, either. Concerned, I think, but sometimes it seemed like she was concerned about what I'd think and other times I couldn't tell at all.

The more I think about this morning, the more I know there's something she's not telling me. I try not to think that it's us or me that she has an issue with. But something is just off and I don't like that she's not telling me.

I hover over my phone for a minute or two thinking about what I want to say. I want to reassure her that I'm fine with how the morning went, and that I'd take her to another movie at the drive-in in a heartbeat. At the same time, I want her to know that I know something's going on and she can tell me.

I hesitate though; I have the feeling it'll only make her feel guilty, and that's the last thing I want. I pry just a touch.

Griffin: *Glad to hear it. Are you sure everything's okay for your shift? I can get someone to cover you, if you need*

I send the text and wait, prepared to cover her shift myself.

If none of the other wait staff wants to take her shift, then I have no problem taking orders and bringing the food out. That's half of running the bar. If everybody else runs into trouble and can't make it, I have to be fully prepared to run the place by myself. I've done it before, and I'd do it for Renee without a second thought.

Renee: *I'm good :) Unless you want me to take the night off so you don't have to see me?*

Griffin: *I hope you're kidding*

Renee: *;)*

I don't know what that wink means, exactly, but I hope it's something good. I debate on texting something else, tapping my phone on the bar, but I decide to let it go. I spend most of the time in the back with the new brew. It's almost ready and smells fucking amazing. Time slips by slowly and when Renee gets to the bar, she gives me a quick smile. It doesn't hide the look in her eyes. It's the same way she looked the night I followed her to the back room. Something's not right.

I only take half a second to decide, and then I go to the back room after her.

Renee's already changed by the time I get there. It makes me think she knew I'd follow her, because she turns around as soon as I step through the door with a forced smile on her face.

"Hey." I smile back at her because I can't help myself. "Everything going okay?"

"Of course it is." Renee's smile drops, but only for a split second, and then it's back in place, never once reaching her eyes. "Is everything okay with you? You seem worried."

I'm worried about her, but it's crossing a line to insist that she tell me what's bothering her. "Everything's great with me. If you need anything, you'll tell me, right?" I try to stress it to her, because she's honestly freaking me out with this back and forth and I don't know what else to do.

Renee takes a breath. "I could do that, yeah."

I brace for her to add something about pretending that I'm the kind of guy she can call in a pinch or pretending that we're together and not just pretend dating, but Renee just nods.

She corrects herself. "I'll do that I mean. If I need anything, you'll be the first person I ask," she reassures me and then offers a small smile. This one seems more like her. More like everything really is okay.

I take a steadying breath. "Good," I tell her and then add, "I don't mean to..."

"No, I know. I'm just a little off with some stuff on my mind," she says and then waves her hand. "Nothing for you to worry about."

"You're sure?"

"Stop," she says with a playful smile. "You make me smile." Propping herself up on her tiptoes she kisses me right then and there and it's unexpected. When she sees it gets to me, she does it again and I love it. Small pecks of reassurance.

"You make me smile too," I tell her and then I have to get out of here, because if I stand in the back room for another second I'm going to close the door behind me, lean her up against it, and kiss her until she begs me to take her to my place.

Even though it's a Monday, it's busy. People are amped up for the holidays and having relatives in town, so there are a few louder tables with groups who are catching up after a few months apart. I don't have much time to watch Renee, much less talk to her. She lights up all her tables, as usual. I catch her eye across the bar a few times, and every time it happens, she smiles at me.

It's a small, private smile, and it reminds me of last night. Somehow, last night feels like it was a year ago or more, and I've been wondering about her ever since. The pull between us is stronger than ever. If I can get a spare minute, I'm going to take her aside in the break room and ask her if we can talk after I close. Even if all I can do is kiss her, that'll be more than enough.

Knowing I have a plan makes it easier to get through the rest of the shift. I'm dead set on making sure she knows I'm here for her, and that everything's more than okay. I know how Renee melts into me when we kiss and how quickly it can go from innocent to hot. It's purely about making sure she's okay. Whatever this is on her mind seems like it's more serious than she's letting on.

About an hour before closing, she comes over to talk to Patty at the opposite end of the bar. By then, all her tables are mostly closed out, just finishing the last of their drinks. Patty nods at her and reaches out to pat her shoulder, and I'm distracted by a customer at the bar needing a drink, and by the time everything is said and done, Renee's nowhere to be seen.

"I let her head out early," Patty says when she catches me looking around. "Said she had a few things to do tomorrow, needed the rest."

"Oh. Okay."

"Hope that's okay with you." Patty frowns at me. I'm usually the one who lets people off early if I'm working at the bar. "I didn't mean to step on your toes. I'm sorry if I did."

"No, no," I'm quick to reassure her. "Patty, that's fine. I'm good." I smile at her, big as I can, and keep that attitude with me until it's time to close.

I don't hear from Renee that night, and I don't expect to. If she has things to do in the morning she'll be in bed. But damn if I don't want to drive over to her place. It just doesn't feel right, and I play back that moment in the back over and over rather than sleeping.

The next day, it's me and Brody behind the bar, getting things ready for the day, both of us tired from the women in our lives keeping us up at night. His exhaustion is warranted...mine is not. We work in relative silence although he does ask me how Renee is doing.

I keep it light and say it's all good even though it doesn't feel like it is.

I texted Renee after I worked out but didn't hear anything back. When I have things set up for the first customers, I send her another message.

Griffin: *Hey little tease…I'm missing your smiles today.*

I'm almost sure that will get an answer out of her, maybe even a laugh, but my phone doesn't go off. *Fuck*, I can't shake this feeling and I don't know why.

Brody makes small talk and for once I just can't focus on anything, not even the damn weather.

My fingers itch to text her again, but I don't let myself take my phone out of my pocket. I'm not going to be the kind of guy who bothers her because she didn't answer two text messages.

"Christmas is coming up." Brody folds his arms over his chest and looks out the front window of the bar. Most of the snow blew away already, but the town still has a holiday look about it. There are garlands everywhere and most of the businesses have a wreath on the door. "You're going home, right?"

"Yep. Visiting with my parents. I'm going to stay for a couple days if that still works out for you."

"It'll be fine. I'll manage the bar the day after Christmas. I figured we could do a short shift just so people have somewhere to go, but I don't want to keep everybody here too long."

"Sounds like a great plan. It'll be my turn next Christmas when you have the little one."

"I'll hold you to that." Brody smiles, but it takes him a few beats to turn and smile at me. I know he's thinking of Mags and his new family. By next Christmas they'll have a baby who's about a year old. His life will look completely different. He must be thinking the same thing, because he says, "I can't wait."

We stand there for a minute with him checking his phone and me avoiding checking mine because I know she hasn't messaged. The guys in the kitchen are making noise, getting ready, and I can hear Mary Sue on her phone in the break room, talking to somebody before her shift.

Frustration gets the better of me and I pick up my phone before I've finished the thought and send her another message.

Griffin: *Just thinking about Christmas plans. Is there anything you like to have on Christmas in terms of food?*

There's another pause that's so long that we get our first customer up at the bar. I pour his drink, and Brody chats with the guy, taking over the tab when my phone goes off in my pocket.

My heart drops when I see it's just my mom. I read her text and I know she just misses me. A second comes through before I can respond to the first.

Mom: *I can't wait for you to come home. I'm making your favorite cookies. Do you want sweet potatoes and mashed potatoes at dinner? I don't mind making both.*

Mom: *Your father is telling me that he wants both. Sorry to bother you I hope your morning is going well*

Griffin: *You're not bothering me at all and I'll eat both kinds of potatoes. Love you Mom. Have a good day*

I hit send on the last message to my mom. Before I can put my phone away, Renee's name pops up on my screen.

Renee: *I can't go*

I open up the text fully and read it again. She can't go? The only plans we have are for Christmas. My stomach turns into a knot. I don't know whether to be worried that something happened, or worried that she's changed her mind about me, or worried that some other thing happened that's about to completely blindside me. Maybe her family decided to celebrate this year, I don't know.

Griffin: *To Christmas? Everything okay?*

She doesn't answer.

I run my fingers through my hair with frustration. I'm ruining this and I know it but all I want is for her to talk to me. But I think that's the last thing she wants.

I get the feeling that it's over. And I hate it.

Renee: *Yeah, I can't come because something came up.*

I'm sorry.

She responds an hour later.

Griffin: *It's all right. How are you doing?*

Renee: *I miss your smiles today too.*

I stare at my phone feeling like there's hope and like I need to stop pushing. I'll just be here for her because I know she's going through something. I just don't know what. I can make her smile though.

For a moment I feel like it might be okay.

If only I knew what was coming.

CHAPTER 16

RENEE

I'm so disappointed in myself that the emotions won't stop hitting me. Every time I breathe through it, they just come back again. I'm not totally sure what feels worse. Disappointing Griffin or not being able to do a damn thing to really help my mother.

There's only about two thousand dollars in that water jug at home. That won't last her very long, and I'm not sure she'll even accept it.

I tried to give it to her this morning, and she flat out refused.

I can barely think of anything else. Other than Griffin.

He's too sweet and understanding, and somehow that makes it all worse. I feel like I'm using him, and I feel like he knows that. It's awful. I stare at the bottle of wine, nearly empty now, and I know I should tell him that I can't do this right now. It's all me and not him. Tears burn my eyes. I don't want to. Not for one second. But I can't keep doing this to him and I can't tell him what's happening. My mother's story is hers. Her pain is so fresh and fragile, and I don't trust this town or anyone in it to help her get peace.

Even if she doesn't get a happily ever after, she should at least have peace. I can help her get that. I have to.

I write out so many messages but I don't send any.

I'm sick over it all and the one person I wish I could cry to, I just can't. I can't tell Mags and drag her down. Not when she's so close to delivery and going through so much already. I've never felt like a weak person, but I have felt this helplessness before. So many times for the same reason, but this time feels heavier.

Maybe I don't have to end it yet, but won't that make me a worse person? Because I'm falling for him, and I think he's falling for me and none of this will ever work. I know it. I know I'll never be the person he deserves, not when I have to hide so much of who I am.

I think we should go back to pretending, because if this gets too real, I'm going to fall apart.

I type the message out, then delete it. Then I type it up again and send it.

I don't want to explain to him what's really going on. I don't want him to know that about my family and I don't want to explain to him what my mother's been through.

Part of getting my fresh start and putting my life back together was supposed to be that I got to leave the past behind. I didn't want to be the girl who wore it all on her sleeve. I know I could just say that I have to be with my mom for Christmas, but Griffin is the kind of person who will care. He'll want to know more about her. He'll ask questions.

And I might give him answers. I like him enough and want him enough to want to tell him the truth. A part of me is dying to tell him because I feel like somehow he'll just know how to fix it. He seems to know how to fix that part of me deep down inside that's been hollow and aching for so long. But what if I tell him and he sees just how broken I am?

What if...what if...what if...what if. All the what ifs keep me company in my empty apartment along with messages from Griffin.

He's too good for me and I know it. I want to tell him, but he has to already know and if he doesn't, I don't want him to see that. Not yet.

I'm still on the couch under my blanket, hiding from life, when there's a knock at my door.

I jump off the couch, startled, and drop my phone into the cushions. He didn't come over, did he? Did Mags somehow know something is wrong and decide to drop by? Is my mom okay?

I didn't realize just how much the wine had gotten to me until I stand up too quickly.

"One second," I call, then rush over to the kitchen sink in record time and wash my face so it's not too obvious I was crying. Then I head to the front door.

I look through the peephole, and my heart drops. It's Griffin, standing outside the door to my apartment with his hands in his pockets.

I unlock the door and pull it open, aware of the puffy skin around my eyes. His eyes widen when he sees my face. He knows I've been crying. Washing my face in the kitchen sink didn't help at all. I hoped it would do a little better job than that, but it's too late.

Griffin looks into my eyes for a beat, and then he shakes his head. "What happened, Renee? I didn't mean it. Whatever I said, I didn't mean it. Whatever I did. I don't know what it was, but I didn't mean it because I'd never want to upset you."

"What?" I have no idea what he's talking about. "You didn't say or do anything."

He glances around the hallway. "Can I come in?"

"Of course." I hold the door open for him, then shut it behind him. When I turn around, he's given me a little space in the small foyer, his hands still in his pockets. "Griffin, I don't know what you're talking about."

He looks at me, his eyes dark with emotion. "Whatever I did that made you change your mind, I didn't mean it."

It takes me a minute to even remember which text I sent him. Which truth I unveiled. My eyes sting but I swallow down every bit of emotion. I wish he just knew. Wouldn't it be so much easier if I didn't have to betray my mother or open up every little part of me that wants to stay hidden. I wish he just knew.

"You didn't do anything." My throat gets tight with more tears, but I swallow them down. Now is not a good time to start crying again. Griffin furrows his brow. He obviously doesn't believe me. "Griffin, I mean it. You didn't do anything wrong. You've been great."

"You're talking about Christmas, right? You can't come with me to my family's Christmas?"

I blink away all my thoughts. Is this about dinner? About the Christmas dinner? It seems so...not as heavy. Words evade me as I try to make my brain work right. "I can make that up to you," I say, although I don't know how. It's important to him I'm sure. In ways it never was for my family. In ways that are different from the things I'm going through. I didn't think he'd care this much, but for him to look at me like the way he is over turning down an invitation, it meant more to him. I can see that. *Shit, shit, shit.* I wish he just knew.

I want to go with him so badly that I almost backtrack, but I can't do that to my mom. Not after everything she's done for me. Not when she's so close to being safe for the first time.

"I can go with you on Christmas Eve," I offer quickly. More words try to follow, with more explanations, but I focus on the main point. "But I want to be with my mom for Christmas."

I almost make it through without giving myself away, but my voice hitches on the word *mom*, and Griffin's eyes fill with more compassion. It's exactly the face I thought he'd make, and my heart aches to see a piece of recognition in his gaze. I clench my teeth together so I don't blurt out all the reasons I have to be with her and how this year's different.

"Okay," Griffin says, a tentative smile spreading over his handsome face. "That sounds good. I want to be with my family on Christmas, too. I can meet your mom on Christmas Eve or are we preten-?"

"No," I say, too quickly cutting him off. It's only after I've shut him down that I realize he might have been joking. My heart races and I wish he'd leave now. I fixed it. *I fixed the problem; please go before I make more mistakes. Please leave before you see too much.*

He blinks, shocked, and I can tell he's thrown off. The silence between us feels tense in a way it's never felt before. I hate having to tell him no. I hate having to keep that part of my life separate from whatever it is that Griffin and I are doing, but that's how it has to be. I can't let him that far in, otherwise I'll never be able to leave it fully behind.

Because Griffin grew up in a good home with good parents, and he'll want me to have the kind of life he does now. That's just not possible. I can have a nice life with my mom, but I'll always be the girl who got my mother's life completely off track. I'll always be in danger of doing that myself. Falling too hard for the wrong guy. Asking too much from the wrong people. Not fighting hard enough until it's too late. Every little voice in the back of my head that kept me up at night for the last year screams at me.

"Renee." Griffin's voice is so gentle that tears come to my eyes again. I blink hard until they're gone, but he's patient, still waiting for me. "What happened?"

"I don't want to talk about it. I'm still dealing with some things."

I move past him into the living room. I'm mostly

expecting that he'll leave, so I keep moving. I find the remote on the side table and sit down on the couch. Pulling the blanket over my lap feels like putting on soft armor.

But Griffin doesn't leave. He turns around and watches me for a few long seconds, then shrugs his coat off. He steps around in my entryway, taking off his shoes and hanging up his coat, and then he pads into my living room, his gaze moving over my couch and my small coffee table and my low bookshelf.

"You have a nice place," he says.

"Thank you. I like it, too." The truth is, I like it even more now that Griffin's standing in it. And...I want to leave it, too. I want to leave my whole life behind and find a place that's never been part of my history or part of running away from the past. "You want to sit down?"

"Yeah, I do." He sits at the end of the couch, then takes the side of my blanket and pulls it over his lap, too. I want to lean into him and let him put his arm around me, but that tension is still there between us, and I feel like I'm about to break down. "Renee."

I look at Griffin. There's only about a foot of space between us. He could lean over and kiss me right now, and I'd probably fall right into the couch. I'd let him take me to bed. I want him to take me to bed, but if I let my guard down, I'll spill all my secrets.

"Yeah?" I ask, after a silence that feels loaded with all the things we've done together. It's not much, compared to what other couples like Mags and Brody have done. Griffin and I haven't had a relationship that's official in the eyes of the town. We haven't moved in together or decided to have a baby together or gotten married. Still, the things we *have* done suddenly seem to mean much more than I ever thought they would.

"Can I do anything for you?"

He's too kind. This man is just too kind. The last time I spiraled was when my mother went back to him. After I said I couldn't. After I begged her not to. And it feels so close to that happening again. He shouldn't have to see that.

"It's okay. Whatever it is, just don't shut me out okay?" he says without me saying a word. Like he can read my mind. Like he just knows.

My heart breaks into a million pieces but I swear every shard falls right into his lap. Like the pieces always belonged to him and never to me.

I can only nod and then scoot closer to him. I ask quietly, hoping it'll be enough. "Want to watch a show with me?"

"Yeah," he answers quietly, his eyes narrowed and a look there that tells me he's searching for something.

"It's okay if you have to go to work, I—" I start but he

cuts me off.

"I don't have to go to work," he says. I swallow thickly and nod.

I still have the remote in my hand, and I point it at the TV and turn it on. All the apps appear on the screen and I flip to a streaming channel. The show I want to watch is there in the top row so I can continue watching it with zero effort.

I click *play Season One, Episode One* and the theme song starts playing.

Griffin watches me, but I keep my face turned toward the TV. After a few seconds of the old sitcom playing, Griffin scoots across the couch like I did, each of us moving a little toward the other until our legs are touching under the blanket. He reaches for the remote in my hand and sets it aside. Then he takes my hand over the blanket and squeezes it gently in his. He waits for the theme song to end before he speaks.

"Why are you watching this?"

Another wave of tears comes to my eyes, but I blink them away quicker this time. It's the fact that he's here now that's making me emotional. It's how he asked me about the show with no judgment in his voice.

I want to tell him everything, but I can't, so I decide to tell him something. *What if he judges my mom?* What if...what if...what if...all those what ifs yell in the back of my head, telling me to shut up. Just part of the truth because he's here with me and he wants to know.

I clear my throat, and Griffin squeezes my hand again.

I squeeze his hand back. "I used to watch it when I was little, and it always made me feel better."

He nods, still watching the TV. Griffin waits another minute or two before he leans over again, keeping his voice low so he doesn't talk over the show.

"Are you going to tell me what happened?"

I keep my hand in his because I don't want him to think I'm angry. Well—I *am* angry, and I'm sad, but I'm not angry at Griffin. None of this is his fault.

And I don't want to lose him. I desperately don't want to lose him, but I don't want him to hurt like I do.

"No," I tell him. "Is that okay?"

Griffin runs the pad of his thumb over the back of my hand. "For now," he says.

CHAPTER 17

GRIFFIN

One episode of Renee's favorite show plays on the screen. A second one starts automatically, and Renee doesn't move to stop it. I'm sure as hell not going to leave her alone right now, but it's just so off. All the little things that have made her seem so unhappy circle around in my head. The last-minute appointment. Seeming sad at work.

What the hell happened and more importantly, why can't she just tell me?

And when she opened the door to her apartment tonight, her eyes were red, like she'd been crying for a long time. She's vulnerable and I don't know what to do to make it better.

So I just wait, hoping any second she'll say something. She'll give me a clue or tell me what to say or do. All she does is scoot closer, hold my hand tighter, occasionally give my hand a kiss, and when she does I lean down and kiss the top of her head.

It's heavy and deep and I know it's been happening for a little while at least. Did someone die?

Another episode starts, and all I can think about is how we started.

She wanted to pretend. And I went along with it, but it's not all a lie.

I felt the way she kissed me.

It had to be real. When she said she wanted to come to my place, and the way she acted once we were there...I could have sworn it was real. I might have played it safe when I told Brody about it, but I didn't really think there was a chance it was all an act. I couldn't see the point in pretending something like that when we were so good together.

Now I'm starting to have my doubts.

But this right here...it has to be real. I almost tell her I don't want to pretend, but I am scared to say the wrong damn thing.

I put my arm around Renee's shoulders and steal a

glance at her to see how she is. But I can't tell. Her eyes stay on the TV. Every so often they look shinier, like she might cry, but she just breathes deep, blinks, and never lets a tear fall.

That feels as wrong as when she let her sadness show on the way into her shift, and as wrong as it felt when she looked at me in the break room and told me everything was fine with that beautiful but fake smile.

"Renee," I say, meaning to get her attention so I can ask her what's really going on. I don't know what the magic words are to get her to understand that she can trust me.

"Hmm?" she answers, and she sounds distant, but there's a bit of warmth there that I needed. Something to just hold onto.

"You know whatever it is, you can walk away from it. You can—"

"There are some things I can't walk away from," she says, not waiting for the rest of what I was going to say. "Things I won't be able to change no matter what I do."

"You could tell me what those things are." I rub my hand up and down on her arm. "Holding it in sometimes makes it worse," I offer but she doesn't say anything. "I've heard I'm a decent listener."

"You own a bar," Renee says, laughing again. It's a sad, soft laugh. "You're a bartender. Bartenders have to be good listeners."

"You're a good talker," I tell her. "Everybody smiles when you come to their tables." Every beat in my chest is a dull thud. She's so fucking broken down.

She bites the inside of her cheek, her eyebrows pull together, and for a second it just seems hopeless.

"Some stuff I just don't talk about." Renee turns her head and looks me in the eye. There's determination in her expression. "And I'm not going to talk about it even if somebody keeps asking. Even if that means you don't want to stay. I just can't talk about it."

I'm not afraid of whatever secret she's keeping, or whatever she's sad about. Things happen to people in their lives. People have rough patches and dark moments and things they carry around like a burden that sometimes only get put down when they're posted up at a bar. I'd carry Renee's burden, no matter what it was.

I am afraid of losing her though. Either from me asking too many questions or because she breaks herself down. "I'm not pushing."

"It seems like you might be," she says lightly, and turns back to the show but leans less on me, literally putting space between us.

"Renee."

"Yeah?" She glances at me out of the corner of her eye. It's a guarded look. Her eyes are still rimmed red, and her cheeks tear stained no matter how much cold water she splashed on them.

"I like kissing you. Do you know that?"

There's a small reprieve in her stare. Renee gives me a breathy laugh. "You've said that before."

"I used to wonder what it would be like to kiss you all the time, and then I found out. It's hard to stop thinking about it."

She turns her face another inch toward me, the TV reflecting in her eyes. "Is there something you want to ask me, Griffin? Something different from...the questions I don't want asked?"

There are tons of things I want to ask her. The questions pile up and I shut them all down.

Instead I pretend we're back at the drive-in movie, and I'm just flirting with her because it's date night. I pretend because it's what she asked me to do.

"Would you mind if I kissed you now?"

Renee shakes her head, and I swear I watch her walls fall down around her. Just like that night in the break room. Just like that moment at the bar.

I reach over and take her chin in my hand, then pull her face toward mine. Touching her is a balm to the pain that I can't stop. Renee leans into my arm around her shoulder and lets me tip her face up and kiss her. Deep and slow. The warmth is overwhelming.

She needed this. Hell, I needed it too.

She tastes sweet and a little salty, like some of her tears got on her lips and dried there. It takes her a minute to let me in, and then she kisses me back slow and deep. Her arms come up and circle my neck, and I tip her against the arm of the couch and hold her while the show plays on in the background. She tastes so damn good and feels perfect in my arms, and at the same time, I keep thinking this is wrong. There's something wrong. She's hurting too much for one person.

There has to be a way to get her back.

I keep kissing her until she gasps and leans her head on my shoulder, and then I just hold her.

"I'm really tired," she says, after a while. "I think I need to go to bed early tonight."

"Do you want to take tomorrow off?" I ask her. "Sleep in, rest up?"

I expect for her to argue with me because she's always looking for extra shifts. Renee almost never turns them down. I know she's saving up and trying to get ahead, but she can't come in like this.

"Okay," she agrees.

We finish the episode of her show, and then Renee walks me to the door, saying she needs to sleep. When I ask if she wants me to stay, I already know she's going to say no before she does. I don't want to leave, but I don't want to push. She's so close to the edge already. I bend down to kiss her on the way out, and I get a glimpse of Renee's eyes with an emotion in them I can't name.

She gets up on tiptoe and kisses me on the cheek. Renee makes a little sound as she lowers herself back down, one that might mean she wants more, but she turns away and closes the door behind me.

CHAPTER 18

RENEE

I'm so emotional that I can barely sleep, and when I do, I sleep way too late and wake up with bright winter sunlight coming through my window. I know I've screwed up my sleep schedule already, but I really needed to sleep without dreaming.

When I get to my phone, after a bit of coffee, I have a missed call from my mom and three text messages. They're all about the divorce lawyer, so I get out of bed, shower, and rush through getting ready. The second meeting is almost as bad as the first. My mom looks tired with her lips in a thin line.

I keep thinking...she's not going to go through with it. I'm back and forth with hope and hopelessness. Everything inside feels empty when I look at her. Her black eye is only a rim of darkness now. But she looks worse off now than she did when I first saw her.

"Do you want me to talk to Aunt Laura about coming with you?" I ask when it's over.

She shakes her head. "She already has to live with me while I'm dealing with this. I don't want her to have to see all the dirty details."

"They're not dirty details, Mom. They're your life."

My mom gives me a look, but she doesn't say anything else.

"I wish I did better by you," she nearly whispers as her voice breaks in the lobby. She stops herself from crying and all I can do is hug her harder.

It all happens so fast, yet it feels like every second drags on. All the while every memory of when I could or should have said or done something, like call the cops, plays in the back of my mind. I was only a kid. But I knew it wasn't normal. I knew she needed help I couldn't give her.

"I love you, Mom," is all I can say. I don't have words for any of this. I only have pain and I don't want it, I don't want to give it to anyone else either.

She hugs me goodbye on the sidewalk outside the

lawyer's office and we go our separate ways.

Back home I clean my apartment, then check my bank balances, and take a bath. I have a drugstore face mask to use afterward in an attempt at "self-care."

I end up crying halfway through it and ruining the mask. It almost ruins the rest of the evening, too. I'm drowning in all my emotions but especially the anger. Anger at myself, my mother, and most of all a man who won't ever see consequences for what he's done. After I wash the mask off and sit with a cool cloth over my eyes, my face doesn't look much better.

My phone pings and I stare at it, like I should be angry at it too.

Griffin: *How are things today?*

Renee: *Okay*

With a deep breath I wonder if I should write anything else, but I don't want to. It's like a dam building up when all I want it to do is drain. I think of how I told my mom that her life isn't made up of dirty details, and I feel like a hypocrite.

For the second night in a row, I toss and turn, thinking about everything I could have changed along the way. I miss Griffin so much that I fall asleep way too late again and sleep through my alarm.

Luckily my shift at the bar doesn't start first thing, so I have time to shower and do my makeup. I need it badly.

Especially the concealer.

I'm a ball of nerves on the way to the bar. If Griffin didn't know about my emotional state, I wouldn't be nervous. I could put on my smile and pretend this was my way out. That all those tips will fill that jar and I could use it to buy all my problems away.

But Griffin does know and that makes the smile harder to pull off.

I meant it when I said that there are some things I don't talk about.

I know he meant it when he said he would listen.

But he just can't understand how knowing those things will take over everything else. He'll always look at me differently, and that's not what I want out of my life, or out of his.

Although he's already looking at me differently, and I hate that too. I'm not handling this well, I know that. But that's why I don't want to talk about it, and I don't know how to...fuck. I don't know how to do this. How to deal with all of this without doing it all wrong. I'm trying, but every time I start to deal with it, I just remember everything and then cry all over again.

Twisting my hands on the steering wheel, I prepare myself to just shut it all down. I can do that and it's always been enough before.

I park out by the road and go around the building

to come in through the front. Before I get to the door, I force my best smile on and tilt my chin up. I'm happy today. I'm moving forward with my life. There's nothing to talk about.

When I go into the bar, it's half full with people eating, talking, and drinking. I'm grateful for that. The music's quiet, like it always is in the afternoons, but there's a feeling of excitement, too. We're getting close to the holiday. I almost forgot that. The reminder is a blessing.

I feel him before I see him. All of my thoughts pause and for a moment I'm scared. Griffin's behind the counter. His eyes are on me the second the front door closes behind me, so I make a point of looking at him and smile. The skin around my eyes is all tight from crying, but I push through it.

Please don't ask me. Just pretend.

Griffin smiles back, and I know just from the look on his face that he can see right through me.

Please don't ask me. Just pretend.

He doesn't follow me to the break room this time. He's probably trying to give me some space, because he's a good man, and I know he heard me when I spoke to him last night. He's being careful with me. I know I don't deserve it, but I want to make it up to him.

I don't know how yet but I know I need to. I don't

want to lose him.

With a steadying breath and a decision to have a good night at work regardless of everything else, I head out of the break room and throw myself into my shift. The habits of taking orders and refilling drinks and bringing out food help the time to pass. I catch Griffin looking at me once or twice and I smile at him both times. There's a look in his eyes that makes me uneasy. I want him to lean over me and kiss me by the register with everybody only a few feet away. I want him to forget that I'm upset and just pretend like I do. This bar is my escape but tonight it doesn't feel like it. Because of him.

It's so fucking obvious how much I've fucked up. My hands go numb and it's harder to go about the night, but I keep it moving and do my job.

Mary Sue comes in after a while and works a half shift. Patty's behind the bar, chatting people up and learning all the town gossip. It slows down for a while as the evening gets later, then gets busy again for a solid few hours. I've been up so late the last couple of nights that I feel almost wired by the time it hits midnight. People start to head out. Patty goes home.

There's a weird lull at one thirty when there's nobody in the bar, but we don't close for another ninety minutes. That's when I decide to take my break. I wash my hands in the bathroom and check my makeup, then go into the break room to catch my breath. And to not think. It's harder than I thought; I'm beginning to spiral. I'm overheating in my uniform and my heart is still aching and I wish I could be two places at once for Christmas and I feel bad for my mom and like I'll never make it up to her, and I can't stand it. But that's what he wants right? For me to go to Christmas dinner. And if I could just do that maybe he'd stop looking at me like that.

My name on his lips startles the hell out of me.

"Renee." I put my hand on my chest in shock, and Griffin stands in the doorway to the break room, looking handsome and worried and like a dream come true. "Do you want to pretend you're okay?"

It takes me a second to even register what he said. I blink at him, shocked, because that's exactly what I want to do. I want to pretend I'm okay until nothing bothers me anymore and all this is done and over with and I made it out just fine. Better than fine. I want to make it out with him still wanting me.

"Yes," I say breathlessly. "Do you want to pretend you're not my boss?"

"Hell yes, I do." Griffin kicks the door shut and comes toward me so fast that I barely get my chin tipped up before he gets there. His hands are all over me in a second, and his mouth is on mine. I get my fingers in his hair and feel him move against me.

Yes. Please. Please just love me right now.

The guilt I've felt all day slides away when he kisses me deeper. I've never felt so wanted. I kiss him back with everything that I have. Every ounce of gratitude and love. Love. Fuck, I know it's love.

My heart races and my blood heats. There's nobody out in the bar right now, but there are guys in the kitchen, and we can't get caught. Somebody has to be out there, but for the first time I don't care. I just want him to pretend to love me and pretend that everything is just fine.

"Please," I whimper and I don't have to say it. He just knows.

Griffin backs me up to a table at the side of the break room and perches me on it. He pushes up my uniform and undoes my pants and helps me kick them off. His hand runs between my legs. All it takes is one touch to light the desire. He pulls the cloth aside and moves his hips, getting closer. I spread my thighs for him and hold onto his waist while he undoes his zipper.

With lust filling every crevice of my mind, I give him every bit of me. Desperate to love him the best I can.

Griffin puts one hand on the back of my neck and uses the other to line himself up, keeping my panties out of the way with the head of his cock. He pushes into me with ease, and I can't close my eyes. My bottom lip drops, and I can barely breathe as he fucks me like he wants to. However he wants to. He can have me, all of me, like this.

Griffin kisses the side of my neck while he stretches me, holding me in place with one hand on my ass and the other under my knee. I grab on to his shirt and push myself onto him.

"You feel so fucking good," he groans in the crook of my neck. "My little tease," he murmurs as he fucks me harder and deeper.

For a few seconds I can't say anything because he found the perfect angle for me to get some contact on my clit. I writhe against him, heat growing between my legs, and chase the feeling of pleasure that will make it impossible to think at all. Griffin's breath hitches and I love that sound so I keep doing it.

What we're doing is so dangerous and risky that it feels like being drunk. We could get caught any second and maybe that's what makes me come, my release hitting me suddenly.

"Renee," Griffin gasps, and then he picks up the pace even more. He feels even harder moving inside me, his cock twitching, and he curses under his breath. Then he pushes in deep, his hips grinding, and I feel him come. The sensation is my undoing.

I kiss him hard when he does. The way we're moving

suddenly seems loud in the break room. My heartbeats remind me that we could both get in huge trouble for fucking at work, but I'm so relaxed in a way that I haven't been for days.

And overwhelmed with something else. Something I can't name. Something that feels just as delicate.

"How do you do that?" I whisper the question. Like it's a secret and I'm not sure I should tell him.

"What do I do?" Griffin breathes against my neck, planting small kisses there. "What did you mean?"

"You make me forget," I tell him.

Griffin takes my face in his hands and tips my head back. "Tell me everything you needed to forget," he says softly. "Whatever it is, you shouldn't have to deal with it alone."

All the good feelings from the sex melt away.

"I'm fine," I tell him firmly. "That wasn't pretend. I'm okay. And I said I don't want to talk about it."

Griffin's face falls and the gravity of it all comes back too soon. "Renee, I can tell—"

"You don't know what you're talking about," I say, feeling tears brimming and I can't even pinpoint why. Why is it spiraling? Can't we just go back?

He slides away from me and glances at the door like he's just remembered he's my boss. I hop off the table, find some paper towels, and clean myself up while he puts his pants back on.

"I want to know," he says when I turn back around. "I care about you, and—"

"No," I say, too loud and too fast. "No, you don't care about me. Because all of this was pretend. Remember? None of it was real. It was just a way to have fun because it can't go anywhere. This just isn't going to be a thing."

Griffin opens his mouth, but the door opens out front, and I know we're out of time.

"I have to get back to work," I tell him, and leave him in the break room. And my heart stays back there, too. It must. Because for the rest of the night I feel nothing but hollowness, and for the first time with Griffin, like it's a mistake that can't be undone.

CHAPTER 19

GRIFFIN

F *uck. Fuck. Fuck.*

I wait in the break room for ten minutes, trying to figure out what the hell I'm supposed to do. Renee's voice comes back to where I'm sitting from the front room. She sounds happy, and I know it's all for show. It's fake. She's pretending.

But that stuff she said just now wasn't pretend. She meant it. Or she was angry enough to want to mean it. Her eyes flashed when she told me that none of this was real.

Why couldn't I just up and let it be? It's what she asked.

I had to go and ruin it.

With my hands gripping the edge of the desk, I sit there for another few minutes trying to decide what *real* is. Is something only real if the whole town knows about it? Is something only real if everybody in your family and everybody who drinks at your bar approves? Is it only real if you've never been somebody's boss?

Everything feels real to me. She's real and so is her pain. Anger gets the best of me, and I throw the first thing I can get a grip on. The mug that was on the desk shatters against the wall and I don't fucking care.

I love her. I fucking love her. I want her and I need her to know that it's real for me. Why the fuck did I have to say anything? For a moment it was all okay. She was mine and I was hers and everything was okay.

I steady myself before I lose my goddamn mind over this woman.

I can't keep thinking about the what ifs anymore, so I shake it off and go back out to the front. Renee keeps herself busy, not looking at me while she chats with the guy at the bar. He looks tired, like he just needed a drink to finish off the day, and he doesn't stay long.

I feel like I can't breathe. I just fucked Renee in the break room while there were guys in the kitchen and the bar was still open. I don't know what's more real than that. I can still smell her on me. Every time I try to say something to her, the words get stuck on the way out.

I don't know what to do if she won't tell me.

We move around one another like we don't exist.

The guy at the bar finishes his drink, leaves a tip for Renee, and heads out.

With no one else here, Renee and I silently clean the bar for the next day and avoid each other. In the kitchen, the guys give each other shit while they wash everything down. I feel like I could cut the tension between us with a knife.

It only gets worse when I tell the kitchen guys they can head home fifteen minutes early. Every bit of emotion stays just beneath the surface. But not a goddamn word comes to mind to say. Every goddamn thing I do from the moment Renee left me in that room until now when I'm watching the last of them leave is pretend. The only thing that's real is the tension between Renee and me.

The door closes with the kitchen staff leaving.

Then it's just us. In the calm after the storm.

She keeps herself even busier with all kinds of last-minute stuff, barely meeting my eyes. I get it. It hurts to look at her, too, because I don't understand where the hell everything went so wrong.

It matters more than anything, and it doesn't matter at all. I'm not going to fire her. I'm not going to make her stop working at the bar. If she wants to quit, she can, but it's not going to be my choice.

I swallow my pain while we close. Renee heads out before me. It's snowing again for the second time this month. That never happens in Beaufort.

And this? Falling in love with someone this hard? That never happened to me.

I lock everything up and make my way to the bar to tell her I'm sorry. Cause I can at least say that, but she's already gone and is by her car.

I wait a moment, but she doesn't leave. There's a small chance. There's the smallest shred of hope.

Renee's watching me from where she's standing at her car, her red hat setting off her pink cheeks, and gives me a slow, sad smile. And I feel like I already know what she's going to say, and I don't want her to. I don't want this to be over.

I walk through the layer of snow in the slim parking area until I'm close enough to lean in for a kiss. Maybe that will fix everything. Maybe, if I can just kiss her one more time, I can put us back together.

I almost make it. I can feel the heat of her breath and feel how close we are together when Renee stops me with a finger on my lips and a quiet laugh.

"It's over, isn't it? No more reason to pretend," she says, her voice clear and soft through the December air. Is there disappointment in her tone, or am I imagining it? "Besides, you're my boss. Pretty sure you can't do that."

My heart beats hard, sending blood rushing to my face. The beat is loud in my ears now that all the noise from the evening is gone, and...this isn't how I thought this would go. Somehow, I thought...

I want to step closer to Renee, want it so bad I can taste it, but I lean back an inch and kick at some of the rocks that came loose from the snow. I'm just trying to think of what to say but anything I could say will make this worse. The rocks land in the snow that's beginning to cover the dirt road behind the bar where we park.

I stick my hands in my pockets so I don't reach out and touch her. Because she's right. I am her boss, and this never should have technically happened. Half of me wants to anyway. Half of me doesn't care that we were pretending. It's killing me that she thinks we were. That after everything, she still thinks it was fake.

A voice screams inside of me that she's lying and that she doesn't want this to end, but after the last week I have no fucking clue if I really know what's going on in her head.

Renee's body is tucked tight to her car, her other arm over her stomach, and I think about saying it. How hard could it be to tell her the truth?

It was never pretend.

It's late, and everybody in the whole damn world is

asleep, and nobody has to know what we say to each other. Nobody has to know anything, but Renee should know this.

"What if—"

A pair of headlights shine on the snow, and a car rumbles along the dirt road, slow to account for the snow and the late hour. I lean back, but don't let myself take the step. *What does it matter if they see? Why does anything matter except Renee?*

But I can't keep talking when somebody might be staring out the window of their car at us. Renee and I both watch the car go. One of its wheels dips into a groove and spins.

Whoever's behind the wheel revs the accelerator and their wheel pops free of the groove. They keep driving until they're out of sight.

I turn back to Renee, but her eyes are still on the spot where that car disappeared into the night. It's clear the moment was broken by that car. I'm not going to get it back. She bites her lip, looking beautiful and determined, and I'm not sure I like where that look's going. Car or not, maybe I was already too late. Maybe it was never on the table for this to be real.

Renee lets out a little sigh, her breath white in the cold. It dissipates quickly, and I keep my hands pushed into my pockets.

She looks up at me, and it feels like she's a million miles away instead of half a step across a dirt parking area.

"All the what ifs don't add up when it comes to us, Griffin."

There's a beat where I think she might take it back, but her face doesn't fall and her eyes don't soften and she doesn't. She opens the driver's side door of her car and climbs in.

I wrap my hand around the top of the door frame as she puts on her seatbelt. It clicks into place, and I want to reach down and undo it. I could take her hand and pull her out of the car and kiss her. My fingers tighten on the doorframe, but I can't be the guy who holds her door open to keep her here with me.

I have to force myself to loosen my grip.

"Get home safe, Renee."

"You, too." Her hands are on the wheel. She looks up at me, and there's something in her eyes that makes my stomach sink. It makes me sure that someday, she's going to leave this town, and I'm never going to see her again.

I open my mouth to say something. I could tell her not to drive away. I could admit to the feeling that's taking up my whole chest. I could make her promise not to leave town. Cause it feels like I'm never going to see her again.

Based on what? Something she thinks is pretend?

Renee's watching me back, and there's a hint of indecision in her eyes, but then she takes a breath, and I don't want her to tell me to shut the door. I don't want to make her ask me to back away.

"Good night," I tell her, and shut the door.

Renee turns away and reaches for something on the dash. Her headlights turn on, and they splash against the back door of the bar. I turn my back on Renee and stride over to my own car. She looks out her window and lifts her hand to wave to me.

I wave back, hating every second and regretting it all, while wanting it all back.

Then she backs out of her spot, her tires cutting new tracks in the snow, and pulls carefully out onto the road. Renee pauses to make sure there's no traffic, even though there hasn't been another car since the one that drove by, then starts down the road.

I wasn't going to stand here and watch her leave, but that's what I end up doing. Her tail lights flash red a couple of times as she makes her way down the road. I can see her silhouette in the front seat when the moonlight hits her just right. I don't have enough time to watch her before she turns on her blinker, stops, waits...

And goes.

And then she's gone, and the road's dark. Bar's dark. Sky's dark.

I swallow hard, then unlock my car and dig my ice scraper out from the back seat. No ice tonight, but there's a thin layer of snow. I brush it all off the car and watch it fall away, disappearing as it goes. Then I drop into the driver's seat. The leather's cold and feels pretty damn unwelcoming after the warmth of the bar and the warmth of Renee. I pull the door shut behind me, shutting out the wind, and start the car.

I fucking hate this.

Maybe I should have run after her. But every time I do, she runs faster and farther away from me.

"It wasn't pretend for me," I whisper what I wish I'd told her the very first time she said it. It's too late for Renee to hear me, but I have to get the words out anyway. I flick on the headlights and they light up a piece of the empty road, some dark trees, and the rest of the night without her. "I love you, Renee."

I let my head fall back against the headrest.

Nobody heard me say it, but that doesn't seem to matter.

"Fuck," I admit in the silence. "I know I do, and it's not the same for you."

I need her to know I love her. Even if she doesn't love me. I can't not let her know. She broke my heart regardless. It's hers to keep. So she should know.

CHAPTER 20

RENEE

It's still snowing as I drive home to my apartment. Twice in one year. *What are the odds?*

If it snows three times, we could have a white Christmas, if the snow stays long enough.

The snow can't distract me from all that happened today though. I never should have gone into work, and I knew it. I never should have done any of this. Griffin didn't deserve it. I knew from the very beginning he deserved better than me.

My heart hurts as I drive back in silence, but my head is clear in a weird way that scares me a little bit. I left all my emotions in the break room at the bar. The moment I turned my back on him, I turned my back on a part of myself.

The part that still had hope.

I guess I should use this time to make a plan. I can't keep working at the bar, not when I'd have to see him every day. I can't walk in and just smile knowing he sees through it.

But I have to keep working there until I can find another job. If I can. There aren't many jobs here hiring. The numbing pain spreads through me and I let it. It's something to feel at the very least.

I pull into a spot in front of my apartment building and sit for a minute, watching the snow come down on the windshield. I don't have one of those things to clear the snow off it, if this turns into real snow. Nobody needs one very often in Beaufort.

There's nobody in the parking lot. I always check before I get out of the car. It's still and quiet this late at night. I get out, lock the car, and head inside.

The second I shut my front door behind me, all the emotion from earlier rushes back into my chest. It feels like I'm going to drown in it. I've made so many mistakes. And if those weren't mistakes, then doing the right thing doesn't feel right at all.

It's all just a mess. I don't know where to start

cleaning it up, but I know I should be alone when I do it. *He doesn't deserve this.* That's all I keep thinking.

He doesn't deserve this. And he'll find better.

Of course he will. He'll find a sweet girl with a good family and someone who's not fucked up like me. And he'll get his happily ever after.

With tears pricking my eyes, I get my coat off, dropping my purse in the process, and then my hair gets in my eyes when I bend down to pick it up. I fumble for my phone and look for my text conversation with Mags. I just need to talk to somebody who will understand.

I'm typing out the message when I realize it's three in the morning. If she's awake, she's not going to be feeling great or in the mood to talk to me. If she's not, my text might wake her. And she's due any minute.

What the fuck is wrong with me?

"God." I drop my phone back into my purse. "You're okay," I tell myself, pressing my hands to my eyes. "You're going to survive."

For the longest time, I thought that was all I needed to do. Just survive.

A soft knock at my door makes me jump. My heart races again because of the adrenaline rush. I step closer to the door, holding my breath, and look at the peephole.

It's Griffin.

My heart instantly breaks. I lean against the door and

wish he wouldn't do this. He could just let me go and not make this harder than it has to be. I'm terrified that if I let him in, he'll be perfect to me, and I'm so scared that if I don't answer, I'll regret it.

But I'm more scared of using him. Because he doesn't deserve that.

He knocks again.

I unlock the door without thinking and open it, breathing fast. I don't want to start sobbing in front of him, but I'm too emotional to keep everything in.

Words aren't an option so I stand there, waiting for whatever he has to say. Everything hurts looking at him and I want to fall into his arms and just love him the best I can, but I know it's not enough.

"I want to talk to you." He has his hands in his pockets the same way he did before, and his expression is sincere and open and handsome. Although his eyes are riddled with sadness.

"It's late," I point out.

"I don't care," Griffin says. He lifts his chin a bit, completely determined. "And if I went home right now I'd call you as soon as I got there. To be honest I probably wouldn't even leave the parking lot. I'd just call you from my car."

My heart thuds.

Thump. There's the man I love. *Thump*. Who I just

keep hurting.

"Please, Renee. I really want to come inside and talk."

I nod and open the door wider. It creaks like it wants me to know what I've done. Like it has to remind me that I'm letting him in. I step back out of the way and shut the door behind Griffin. I flip the lock on the door, check it twice, and turn to face him.

Now that he's here, I can feel all the tiredness and tension from the day. My feet hurt, even though it wasn't a very long shift, and my neck is sore.

Everything aches as I lead the way into the living room, feeling Griffin close behind me.

Thump. My heart warns me. *Thump.* Don't hurt him. *Thump.* Just let him say his piece, take it, and let him go.

There's a small nightlight near the door that makes it easier to see my way to the table with the lamp. I turn it on to its lowest setting. The light almost reminds me of candle light. It doesn't hurt my eyes.

Griffin lets out a breath as I let myself fall onto the couch and wait for him. He turns around, and I can hear his shoes landing in the entryway as he kicks them off. I pull the blanket over my lap out of habit. As if it'll protect me.

The couch dips and it's then I realize I've been closing my eyes. I open my eyes and watch Griffin get comfortable on the far cushion. He's careful to give me space, but his gaze moves over my body and lingers on my lips before he meets my eyes. Despite all the emotions I've felt over the past two days, nothing matters when he looks at me like that.

"You followed me home from work," I say, because I'm not sure how else to start off the conversation. Griffin should probably be the one to kick it off, but he's being patient and quiet and watching me like I'll give up some of my secrets just because he's here.

"Yeah, I did. I made a mistake back there in the parking lot. And in the break room."

My heart jumps up into my throat. It feels like it's beating too hard for me to stay alive, but I swallow and keep breathing. "Do you regret it all?"

"No." Griffin shakes his head, a smile coming to his face and dropping away. "I don't regret touching you or kissing you or fucking you. Or being with you. I don't even regret that it was at work while the bar was open."

I'm silent. Swallowing down every thought.

"Renee, you know I wouldn't regret anything we did together, don't you?"

"I know a person can come to regret almost anything." I think of my mom and how she always says *I did it for you, Renee.* It's supposed to be a comforting thing, but it's only comforting to her. It's the reason she gives herself to justify going back to a man who destroyed her life.

She said she's sorry and I've said I'm sorry but sorry never fixed anything. "I know you can get caught up with someone who only ever hurts you, and that lasts forever," I say without thinking and then I want to take it back.

Griffin looks confused. "You've never hurt me. And if I did anything to hurt you, I'm sorry. I'm really sorry. But I deserve to know if I did something that hurt you."

I curl my hands up in the blanket, then let it fall back to my lap. "You didn't do anything to hurt me."

"I fucked up though," he says, and I swear I can't breathe. I know I just need to take this and then it'll all be over. I just need to hold on so I grip the blanket tighter.

He takes a deep breath and runs his fingers through his hair. Griffin's obviously thinking about what to say. He's always been choosing his words, I think.

Griffin looks me in the eye. His dark gaze soft and caring.

"I should have told you the truth about how I felt," he says.

"It's fine if you regret—" I say just wanting this part to be over.

"No, Renee. It's not about regret. I don't regret anything."

"It was just pretend," I lie to myself to make it hurt less. "It didn't mean anything."

"It did mean something. It meant something to me."
I stare up at him, wishing he would just end it faster.

"Okay, but...it can't have meant that much to you."

"That much?" he questions, his voice tight with disbelief in his expression.

I want to say *there's too much you don't know about me.* But that would be giving myself away. That would open the door to so many more questions that I can't answer.

"There's too much we don't know about each other for it to have been—"

"I think we know a lot about each other. And whatever I don't know, I can learn. Because this isn't a game to me, Renee. It's not pretend."

And then there's a loud, heavy knock at the door. Keeping me from telling the next lie just to save him from what happens next.

Knock knock knock.

Knock knock KNOCK.

The blood drains from my face. I know exactly who's at the door. Because it's not the first time. This is what happens. I knew there was no hope.

CHAPTER 21

GRIFFIN

Renee turns white as a sheet. The angry impatient knocks keep coming. And she does nothing. They knock a third time as Renee stares at me.

Something in my blood turns cold. I almost say something to the door, but she stops me. The fear in her eyes stops me.

"Renee?" I say softly.

She throws the blanket off and jumps off the couch. Renee sprints through the living room, keeping her footsteps silent, and I bolt after her.

Renee gets to the door a couple of steps ahead of me

and slams a deadbolt into place.

"Renee," a man on the other side shouts. "Renee, I know that was you. Open the damn door."

"I'm not opening the door and you need to leave," she says, her voice shaking.

"Open the goddamn door." The man outside in the hall pounds on the door again. It shakes in the frame, but the deadbolt holds.

It's nearly four in the morning. *What the fuck is going on?*

I watch her stand on the other side of the door, watching it like she's hoping it'll stay there. Stay shut and keep whoever it is on the other side.

"Come back here," I tell her in a voice just above a whisper. "Renee. Get behind me."

She doesn't move. Fear keeps her in place. It dawns on me that she knows who it is.

"Who is that?" I ask her but she doesn't answer.

"Go away," she calls. Her purse is on the floor near the door, and Renee bends down, snatches it and takes out her phone. She doesn't call anyone with it, though. She just holds it tightly in her hand. "I'm not opening the door so go away."

"Who the fuck is out there?" I repeat but I'm not heard over the fucker who's scaring the shit out of her.

"You owe me a fucking conversation," the man shouts.

"You're the one who started all this. You're the one who did this to me. Getting between me and my wife!"

Her voice cracks and her expression falls. The part of her I knew existed when I left comes out. Tears fall freely and she stands right in front of me, staring at the door, screaming, "Leave me alone! I'm calling the cops!"

He pounds on the door. It's so loud that I'm surprised somebody else hasn't come out into the hallway yet. One of Renee's neighbors or a landlord.

"Who the fuck is that?" I say louder and she barely glances at me. She looks back at me with nothing but shame before breathing heavy and facing the door.

"Go away," Renee repeats. "I'm not opening the door."

That makes him punch the door even harder. So fucking hard she flinches. The fists at my side tighten and I scream out, "Get the fuck out of here!"

He doesn't hear though, not over the rampage he throws.

He stops pretending to knock anymore. He slams his fists on the other side of the door, almost screaming in a furious rage. The things he says to Renee make me want to step outside and beat him to a fucking pulp. I reach for the door, but she stops me by throwing her body in front of me. I stop, frozen from the look of pure fear in her eyes.

He shouts her name but all I can hear is her heavy

breathing, about ten breaths, as he pounds on the door again.

There's a long silence.

Renee doesn't move. Her shoulder braced against the door.

I'm left in shock and with the need to go out there, to do something, but I'm here on the other side with her. Watching her barely keep it together.

"Who was that?" I ask when it seems like he's gone. She looks at me with wide eyes. With both sorrow and shame.

She starts to stand up and then shrieks as there's another pound on the door. "Fucking bitch."

"Fucker!" I shout and nearly kick the door as if it'll hit whoever is on the other side. I'm not a violent man but it's all I feel watching Renee cower.

"Please don't!" she begs me. I've never felt so tormented.

Anger spikes in my blood. If she wasn't holding the door knob, I would be out there in a second.

Without knowing what to do, I reach in my back pocket for my phone to call the police, but I don't have it. *Fuck!*

It's worse this time, even louder, and this time I step forward and wrap Renee in my arms. She doesn't turn around, but she puts her hands over my arms and holds on to me. It's all I can do, hold her and stare at the goddamn door. She doesn't say anything when the man shouts at her to answer, which only seems to piss him off more. The doorframe shakes so hard that it starts to come away from the drywall in one corner.

I reach for her phone to call the cops but the moment I do, the banging stops.

Heavy footsteps go down the hall.

Renee and I both stand there, perfectly still, until she steps out of my arms and away from me.

She walks into the living room, does a small circle near her table, and checks her phone. I'm ready to catch her if she falls, or hold her again, or help her calm down. I don't know what to say, and I don't know what to do, but I don't want to reach for her again unless I'm sure she wants it. My heart is beating too fast to be safe. I should have chased after him. I should've gotten a license plate.

I should have done more than I actually did. All of the things I should have done seep into the moment as the shock wears off. All in all, it couldn't have been more than a couple of minutes. Sanity and clarity come back to me slowly.

"Renee, we have to call the police."

She whips her head around, staring at me with wide eyes. "What?"

"We have to call the police. I can make the call since I was in here with you. You have that guy's name, right?"

"Don't call anybody," Renee says, her voice hard.

"We have to." I want to punch that guy so much that it's hard to keep control of my own voice, but I do it. Renee doesn't need another man losing his mind in front of her tonight. "That man was dangerous. He came here to bother you. We have to call the police."

"Actually, we don't have to." Renee says with that same look in her eyes. Her phone is still in her hand, and her chin is quivering. She clenches her teeth and relaxes them. "We don't have to call them, and if we did, the police wouldn't do anything."

"Yes, they would. They would come here and take a statement—"

"No, they wouldn't." Renee lets out a laugh that sounds sad and bitter and angry. "They won't come here."

"Why not?"

"Because he was on the force." She looks like she's going to laugh again, but no sound comes out. Her eyes are shiny and bright as her chest rises and falls harder and faster and I'm terrified for her. "The police aren't going to do anything because he knocked on my door. They never do, no matter what happens."

"He didn't knock on your door, he practically—"

"Tell them that and they'll look at you like you're the problem." She says like it's a fact. Like she's been through this before.

"He can't bang on your door like that. He can't *threaten* you," I stress.

"It's his word against mine, and he didn't do anything I can press charges for."

"The hell he didn't." I take a big breath and let it out slowly, so I don't get loud with her. "He was threatening you. And I heard every word."

"Your word matters about as much as mine does when it comes to something actually happening. It doesn't mean anything. They're not going to do anything. If you call them, you'll only make it worse," she says.

She wipes at her face as I stare back at her.

"Is he an ex?" I ask. Trying to put the pieces together.

Before she can answer I try another solution. "You can get a restraining order." I know people get those. "You can report this incident and use it to get a restraining order."

Renee shakes her head and looks away. "Do you know how hard it is to get one approved?"

"I haven't—"

She cuts me off with that single, sharp word, her body trembling. "You don't know, Griffin. You have no idea."

"I'm not pretending to have personal experience with it, but it's not nothing. If you can—"

"There's no way to fix this Griffin. You don't know what you're talking about," Renee snaps. She paces around the living room again and whirls around to face me. Her eyes are so filled with tears that they're about to spill over.

I'm left standing there not knowing what the fuck to do to make this better.

"You don't have to do this alone," I tell her because I don't know what else to say.

I'll deal with the police if that's what she needs. I'll be the one to make all the calls. I'll go with her wherever she needs to go. I'll sit by her while she makes a report. Anything.

She stares back at me and for the first time looks at me like I am not her savior. Like I'm not an escape. "You don't know because you have a perfect family and a perfect life, and you don't know what it's like to live in a world where this is what happens when your mom tries to leave."

"Renee," I try. "Your mom—"

"I filed a police report once," she says, almost shouting. "I've been through all that. I tried to get a restraining order. I jumped through all the hoops they wanted, and it didn't work. All it did was make him hit my mom harder." My blood runs cold. I don't understand what the hell she's talking about.

"That guy hits your mom?" I thought he was after Renee but knowing that they have another connection beyond that he's out of control and knows her somehow is worse. It's obvious the control and fear he has over her.

Renee laughs again, but there's not an ounce of humor. She's spiraling, and I need to help her, but when I reach my hand toward her, she jerks away from it.

She seems to realize her state and then backs away, attempting to put herself back together.

"Leave," she says. "Please leave."

"There's no way I'm leaving you here alone. I can't leave. Not after that." She has to understand that, at least. It doesn't matter that we've been sleeping together and pretending. I would stay for any of the people who work for me. I would stay for my friends. I would stay for a person I cared about or someone who just needed my help. Fuck, I would stay for a fucking stranger after that shit.

Leaving her here like this would kill me.

"Get *out*," she repeats. "I can't have you here right now. Leave."

Renee takes a step toward me, then another, ushering me to the door.

"I'm asking you to leave." I shove my feet into my shoes.

Renee goes ahead of me and jerks the door open, breathing hard as I go past her.

"I—"

She shuts the door in my face. I can hear her getting

her locks back in place, and then I can hear her walk away from the door. A minute later, water starts to run somewhere inside her apartment.

I sit down and lean my back against the door. It's four in the morning, but I can't leave. I can't do nothing. I don't know what the hell to do, but nothing is right here, and I can't let her go through this on her own.

All I can think though is, *What the fuck was that?*

CHAPTER 22

RENEE

Every time she leaves him, it's like opening up an old wound. I'm grateful this time I got to the deadbolt in time. It never lasts that long. He doesn't risk more than a few minutes of terrorizing me. But it lasts so fucking long after he's gone.

I hate him. I will always hate him. But even knowing that, I don't know what to do with the anger and the pain.

I wonder if he thought my mom was here like she was last time. He doesn't go to my aunt's. I think he knows better than that. I wish he'd give up on coming here.

Even worse than that, I wish Griffin hadn't been

here. I wish he hadn't seen it. I wish he didn't see me at that moment.

I text my aunt, not my mom. It's so late though I'm not surprised that she doesn't answer. Pulling my pillow tight, I try to sleep.

I'm sure I won't fall asleep, but I'm so tired that I do. Thankfully I don't dream, but when my alarm goes off, it doesn't feel like I've slept at all. I have a terrible headache and I want to spend the rest of the day hiding under the covers.

I'm pretty sure I won't be able to fall asleep again because my thoughts won't stop racing.

I drag myself out of bed, strip my sheets, and throw them into the washer. A quick shower fixes the mess that's my hair, and I take my time drying it. I force myself to eat some toast. I'm feeling a little more human by the time I have something in my stomach, and I switch the sheets to the dryer and get dressed. It's still so early that I have time to do a lap around my apartment while the dryer runs. I fold the blanket and put it over the back of my couch and wipe down the counters and tell myself that it's all right. He'll stop. He'll move on and leave me alone.

I hope she really leaves him though. I hope it really ends. I check my phone and my aunt still hasn't seen the message.

The last thing on my list is to make my bed with the clean sheets. Everything's neat and tidy when I put my coat on and grab my purse.

With a hint of fear, I check the peephole first, he's not there. I flip the locks and pull the door open trying to figure out how I'm going to talk to Griffin today.

A man falls into my apartment and onto my feet as the door flies open.

"Fuck," Griffin groans.

I'd jump backward, but he landed on my *feet.* I gasp at the feeling of his weight on the toes of my boots, and Griffin's blinking up at me from the floor. An absolute wreck with stubble along his jaw and darkness under his eyes. He's obviously been asleep.

Against the door. Oh my God. He slept against my door. My heart falls in a different kind of pain at the sight of him in last night's clothes. Rumpled and looking like he's slept even worse than I did.

"Griffin?" I say in disbelief.

"Sorry," he says as he gathers himself. Seeming to wake up right this moment. He pulls himself up by the doorframe and stands up, brushing at his pants. "The floor's pretty hard out here, but I must have nodded off."

My heart stops and I can't believe he's standing in front of me.

"Nodded off? Have you been sitting here all night?"

Griffin shrugs. "Not all night. We didn't get here until after three."

My face heats up with sheer fear. "You can't do that." I almost say, *what if he came back? What would he have done?* I don't know. I don't know, but Griffin shouldn't be there. He shouldn't have to see my father at all. "You can't just sit outside my apartment when you don't know what you're getting yourself into."

"Well, tell me what I'm getting myself into, then!" he says with exasperation. "I want to help you."

"I don't want your help!" I answer just as exasperated.

"Too bad!" he says back, raising his voice.

All I can think is how reckless he's being. I didn't have a choice. But Griffin does.

"He could have hurt you!" I point at him. "You can't sit at my door when somebody like that could come back at any second."

"I think that's a good reason for me to sit outside the door, actually, if somebody's going to come bother you like that."

I feel like I'm going to catch on fire inside my coat, but I don't want to take it off. I don't want to drop my purse. I don't want to be doing this at all. Everything inside of me is ringing; my hands tremble.

I don't know what my father would have done. He's never hit a man before, but when he gets like that....I just...I don't know what I would have done if he'd hurt Griffin.

I can't say a damn thing. I stand there, feeling helpless and hating that this is my life.

Griffin looks back at me, his shoulders dropping as he lets out a long, deep breath. I wouldn't be this patient with me, but there he is, just breathing so he can think of what to say. He takes a few steps into the living room. I back up a step, but I hit the coffee table and there's no more room.

Griffin holds his hand up like he wants to make sure I won't run away. I'm not going to run away from him. I'm not afraid of him. I'm afraid of everything else that has to do with him and my life.

"I'm asking you to help me," he says quietly. "I want to understand, Renee, and I can't understand unless you tell me what's going on. Please. I won't think less of you for having things to deal with in your life."

"You will." *And you'll judge my mother.* Everyone does. Even I do and I hate myself for it.

"I won't." He shakes his head, his eyes sincere. I can't believe him though, because he doesn't understand what he's asking. "I really won't. I could never think less of you, no matter what you tell me."

"It doesn't matter; I don't want you to—" I start but he cuts me off.

"You matter to me."

"But I don't want..." My voice cracks, and a few tears spill out of my eyes. I wipe them away, but more come after them. "I don't want your help. I don't need your help. I'm never going to need anyone."

Then I can't deny that I'm crying. There are more and more tears, and my chest fills up with sobs, and then I'm just breaking down in front of him. Yet again.

"I don't need anyone," I say, and it sounds like a lie.

Griffin steps forward. I take a breath and I can smell the spicy scent of his cologne leftover from yesterday.

He puts his arms around me, and my whole body seems to break. It's the worst feeling I could imagine, because I can't hide it, and that means Griffin is going to know.

I push my face into the front of his coat and sob. "You can't do this," I tell him.

"Why not?" He rubs my back, his strong arms circling me. There's no way I can tear myself away now. I need this too much, and it's embarrassing and horrible to have to admit it.

"Because now you know."

"What do I know?"

His voice is steady and warm, and I feel even more ridiculous because I could have had this last night. I could have had him with me all night, and it wouldn't have made any difference because he still knows everything anyway. He's a smart man. He'll put the pieces together. He'll ask Brody who will ask Mags.

"You know how damaged I am. You can see how screwed up my life is. And you know that you're so much better than me, and that's why this can never work. You're so much better than me. You don't deserve this."

"Hey," he says, and I cry harder. My purse falls off my arm and onto the floor, and I put my arms around his waist and hold on tight. "It's all right," he says soothingly.

I brace myself because I'm sure he's going to tell me that he's not better, and I can't have that discussion with him right now. It's not really about me as a person next to him as a person. It's my entire life up against his. He has a good family. He can bring someone home for Christmas without having to explain the disaster they just got out of. He won't have to tell anyone that his mom is living with his aunt because of the monster who showed up at my door. He's good, and I can't be good like that.

But Griffin doesn't say that. He doesn't argue with me.

"I'm here," he says, and drops a kiss to the top of my head. "I'm here, and I love you."

I love you.

I take a shuddering breath. I don't know how he can, but I take it. Because I love him, and I need him even if

I don't want to.

"I love you too," I sob, and it's not pretend at all. As much as it hurts, it's real.

I love him and I want him to love me.

Chapter 23

Griffin

I don't know how long it lasts, and I don't try to keep track of the time. I just hold her until she's able to stop crying. She trembles in my arms and I can't believe she tried to go through this alone.

Finally, Renee looks up at me with tear stains all over her face. "I don't think I can cry anymore," she says with a tired laugh. "I think that was all the tears I had in me."

"It's okay if you have more."

"I don't." She shakes her shoulders. "God. I'm sorry you have to see me like this."

"I love seeing you like this," I say without thinking.

She frowns up at me and I clarify. "I don't like seeing you sad." I stroke her cheek with my knuckles. "But I'm glad you can be sad in front of me."

Renee lets out a shaky laugh. "That makes one of us."

I sit her down on the couch and take her coat off.

There's no fucking way either of us is going in today. Bar is closed. We'll blame it on the weather.

I bring her a wet paper towel and wipe her face. I get her some Tylenol and a glass of water, and then I convince her to take a nap. She just needs some rest, and she'll feel so much better. She doesn't kick me out this time.

That's progress.

Renee falls asleep almost as soon as she puts her head on the pillow, and I tiptoe out, closing the door gently behind me. I shower in her apartment and make myself look less like I slept in a hallway all night and get out just in time.

My dad texts me back. I messaged him last night to tell him what was going on. I told him and Brody. That shit can't happen. There's no fucking way I'm going to let that ever happen again.

Renee was wrong about me being better than her. I don't know where she got the idea that she's not good enough for me. She's perfect, and I'm just a guy who had a lot of lucky breaks in life.

I was especially lucky to have parents like mine.

And lucky enough to know people who can make problems like her father go away. Brody filled me in on details I imagine Renee wouldn't ever want to say out loud.

I want that bastard gone. Out of her life. Out of her mother's life.

Fucking gone. My phone pings as I stand by the counter waiting on coffee.

Robert: *Yeah I know her father. And I've heard things.*

I text back and forth with Robert and Brody. My Dad gives me his contacts and I feel somewhat better as the hour passes.

It's not much later when I hear Renee stirring in the bedroom. I knock before slipping in. She stretches out on the pillow, her face pink, blinking herself awake.

"Hey." I sit down on the edge of the bed and run my hand up and down her arm. "Feel any better?"

"I don't have a headache anymore." Her cheeks get redder. Staring down at her, I can't fucking believe she kept it all to herself. Hell, the very moment I had an inkling as to what was going on, I reached out to everyone I knew for help. She shouldn't have to take this on herself. It's eating her alive. She murmurs, "But I'm pretty embarrassed. I'm sorry for acting that way in front of you."

"Don't be." I lean down and kiss her forehead,

brushing her hair out of the way. It's only then, warm on her bed that I realize how fucking tired I am.

Renee smiles a little, but then the smile fades.

"Hey," I whisper and then remind her, "I love you."

She gives me a small smile and says, "I love you too."

The light coming in through Renee's bedroom window is the kind of late-December light that reminds me of the days before Christmas break in school. It reminds me of feeling like I couldn't wait for the last class to get out so that Brody and I could go hang out at each other's houses. I was never worried about anything happening when I was at home, and I want Renee to have that, too. It's a little different now, but there's no reason she and her mom can't have peace in their lives.

There's no reason at all that Renee can't live in her own place without somebody coming to the door in the middle of the night and acting like a violent animal.

I wait for her to be ready. There's still snow outside on the ground, which is a sight that nobody in Beaufort can count on seeing every year. It seems like a hopeful sign. If Beaufort can have this much snow in a single December, then Renee and I can make it. I can help her with what she's going through.

"I can't help thinking that it was my fault," she whispers, like it's a secret. Then she told me everything. Half of me thinks she thought I'd run. That her baggage was too much. But I've fallen for her head over feet and there's nothing she could say that would make me run. Not when I have all of her. I never want to let her go.

"It's not your fault," I tell her, brushing the hair from her face. The bed creaks as I lay down next to her. She makes room under the covers for me.

"I mean...she kept going back to him. Every time she'd leave, he would convince her to come back, and she always said that she was doing it for me." I hold her closer, and she presses herself against me, letting me hold her, my front to her back.

I wish I knew how much she was hurting.

"That doesn't mean it was your fault. It means she loves you, and she didn't have any better options. Or she thought she didn't."

"It feels like my fault sometimes," Renee says, just above a whisper. "Feels like she could have had a better life if I had just...convinced her that I'd be okay, maybe."

"It's not your fault," I promise her. "I have to tell you something." My heart pounds with worry.

"What?"

"My parents drove down today." I don't tell her it's because I messaged my dad. I don't tell her more than I need to, just for the moment.

She stiffens slightly but then relaxes. "If you have to go, that's okay."

"Kind of the opposite of that," I manage. "I know it's not Christmas, but they'd love to meet you."

"I don't know that right now—"

"I told my dad. He's a cop, Renee. He can help." She goes still, staring straight ahead. "They...want to help." I spit it out, even though I know she might not like it. "They just want to make sure you're okay."

"What did you tell them?" she asks, still beside me.

"That I needed help and that I love you."

The bed groans as she looks over her shoulder at me. Her eyes meet mine and a mix of emotions stare back at me. "I told them I love you," I repeat.

Renee wrinkles her nose, attempting to make things lighter when the topic is so fucking heavy. "Did you tell them I'm a wreck?"

"You're not a wreck," I whisper back and kiss her. When I pull back her eyes are still closed so I kiss her again.

"Just tell me you love me," I tell her.

"I love you." Her eyes are still closed.

"Now tell me you'll let me handle this," I say, and she opens her eyes then.

I can practically hear her heart pounding.

"Actually"—I smooth her hair back—"you don't have to say that, and you don't have to do anything."

"Griffin?" she says.

"Yeah?"

"I'm scared."

"You can be scared, but you don't have to be. I'm here. I've got you." I promise her. And I mean it.

I fucking love this woman. I love her so damn much.

And she loves me. That's all that matters right now. Everything else, time will heal.

EPILOGUE

RENEE

ONE YEAR LATER

I'll never forget what Griffin said when I asked: *Why did you have to find me when I was falling apart?*

After all this time, I keep going back to that very moment when it felt like everything was coming undone and I looked at him in that backroom and all I wanted was for him to kiss me. Like that would make it all better. And...in a way, it did. I wish I wasn't at my lowest. For so long I thought, if only I'd went for it sooner and kissed him first when life wasn't so rough with my family. But that's not how life works.

He said, "Maybe fate knew I was supposed to be

there to catch you."

Last December lit my world on fire. It burned so much to the ground, but it brought light to so much more. The best of it all is that I fell for Griffin hard and fast, and I can't imagine my life without him.

"Can you believe it?" My aunt says, interrupting my thoughts. "This is the second year in a row we're having a white Christmas." Her tone is upbeat and I'm starting to get used to that sound.

It's Christmas at Griffin's parents' house, and of course everyone's talking about the weather. In this town snow is just as uncommon as in Beaufort, and nobody can believe what good luck we're having. Snow on the ground at Christmas. I've heard multiple people say they hired photographers to get pictures out in the snow with their whole family wearing matching sweaters and hats. It makes me smile just to think about it. Sheer joy at the simple things.

"What are we missing?" Griffin's dad says. He stands at the head of the table, looking over all the food. "Oh! Potatoes."

"Did Mom make both kinds?" Griffin questions, his expression serious, which only makes his dad laugh harder.

His mom makes a face at him. "Of course I did. I made all of your favorites."

Within two minutes, the potatoes are out on the table, and the dishes clack as we pass them around to each other in the grand dining room at Griffin's parents' house. His mom laughed when she showed my mom and aunt around when they arrived for Christmas. *It's too big for the two of us, but now we have an excuse to use it again!* I've been here more times than I can count. Griffin is close to his family and I love it. I love being a part of his family and I love that he's a part of mine.

I don't know how I could have survived this year without him.

It feels so surreal in this moment. Imagining where we were just a year ago. His mom is genuinely thrilled about being able to eat in the dining room, and I can see why. It has beautiful bay windows that look out over the front yard and a dark wood credenza to store the serving dishes, and everything about it feels warm and homey. It doesn't have a fireplace, but it feels like it could.

Honestly, it feels like something out of a movie, or a book about the perfect Christmas. I keep catching myself smiling at the smallest of things. It's like my life could be a dream. Although it doesn't feel like I'll wake up. It feels real.

How did I get so lucky that this is my life? How did I get lucky enough for a man like Griffin to come to my hometown, see me at my worse and still love me? We went public, so to speak, the very week after he found out everything. I didn't have much of a choice, to be fair. Griffin said he'd fix it and asked me to simply let him.

So I did. And I haven't seen my father since, although I know he works two states over now.

I don't know what, exactly, Robert did, but I know he was involved. Same with Griffin's father, who smiles so politely and has the most contagious laugh. Word around town was that I started dating Griffin, Griffin found something out and poof my father was stationed states away and there was a protective order granted for my mother.

I'm not sure that's exactly how it happened, and I've never wanted to ask about the details. All I know is that my mother is safe, I'm safe, and the last year of my life has been transformative. Therapy helps with that too.

It's not to say there weren't bumps in the road. I still have my moments, even though I've forgiven myself for so many things that were so hard to let go of. I'm working through a lot with my mother too; she wants us to be in a better place after everything happened the year before, and I want that too. I love her and she loves me and life dealt us both a less than easy hand.

There was a lot of paperwork for my mother and way too many meetings at the lawyer's office. I didn't go to all of them because my mom suddenly had twice the support she usually does, but it all worked out. Knowing he's gone makes coping through a lot of difficult memories much easier and more manageable.

And my mom and her sister are having the best time living together. Mom doesn't want to date and she's still getting on her feet, but she's finally free of a life that kept her down for way too long. It's a different kind of happily ever after, but it's the kind that has her smiling so much, the wrinkles around her eyes are more pronounced. But as she tells me all the time, she's earned them. Every laugh line was hard fought.

It's everything I could have hoped she'd have. My aunt even found her a job at the local library coordinating the different activity groups that use the meeting rooms there. She helps them come up with events and makes sure there aren't any scheduling conflicts and even sits in on the weekly knitting group meeting. My mom doesn't knit, but she says those ladies know all the gossip that goes on in the town, so it's an easy way to get her bearings.

"You just like gossip," I teased her when she told me. "You want everybody's latest news."

"I love gossip," my mom admitted, her eyes shining as she joked. "I should have been more of a gossip before."

"You'll have to put in extra work and catch up," I joked.

Glasses raise in cheers at the table as Griffin's mom

tells everyone to dig in. My mother sits across from me at the table, her eyebrows raised in excitement as she tells something to Griffin's mom in a hushed voice and the two of them laugh. They've become such good friends. Between us, we have three towns to catch each other up on. I don't think anybody's going to miss out on good old-fashioned gossip at this meal.

I twirl my fork, not paying attention to my dinner, but trying to get caught up in the story my mom's telling to Griffin's mom, who laughs her way through it.

Griffin gently nudges me with his elbow. "Hey."

"Hey," I say back, matching his down-low tone. He's got a forkful of potatoes, and he's grinning at me. "Is everything okay?" I ask when he doesn't say anything else.

"I don't know, is it? You haven't started eating."

A smile pulls my lips up. "I'm just taking it all in." And that's the truth. There's no pretending anymore with us.

Griffin puts his fork down, and my face gets red as he looks me up and down, taking his time to apparently memorize my dark green velvet dress.

"You're staring," I whisper. "If you keep doing that, you're going to get caught." My cheeks heat from the rise of my blush. This man still gets to me. He always will. I love him more than I knew I was capable of loving.

"Then the entire town would know how much I like staring at you."

I let out a laugh at his joke, the entire town already knows that. "Is that all you like?" I give him a look. "Staring at me?"

"And touching you," he says, running his fingers along the outside of my arm, causing goosebumps in the wake of his touch. My smile widens as he adds, "And kissing you. I wouldn't mind—"

"Hey!"

He cuts himself off, laughing.

I tell him, "You can't be dirty at the dinner table." All flushed and flustered, I tuck my hair behind my ear and peek up at our mothers, neither of them seem to be watching. Thank goodness.

"You shouldn't look so hot at the table, then," he says. Shrugging, he adds, "I can't be blamed."

I pick up my fork again, the smile stuck on my face. I couldn't stop it if I tried. I'm too happy. I remember back to before that first kiss and murmur the nostalgia, "You used to look at me the same way in the bar."

"I used to feel the same way about you in the bar."

"I used to feel the same way too," I admit, although he already knows. I think our souls loved each other before we ever kissed. But when our lips touched, it lit everything on fire that made us what we are. He was always my person. Always. I've told him that many times before, but Griffin grins. He never gets tired of hearing it.

"So," he says, after we've both been quiet for a few minutes, concentrating on our food. It's freaking delicious. His mother knows how to express her love in constant texts and warm food. "Did you get everything you wanted for Christmas?"

"Of course I did. You shouldn't have gotten me so many presents. You're going to make everybody else jealous."

"Like who, Mags? I happen to know Brody got Bridget and Braden a truck full of gifts. I bet it was more toys than they have at the North Pole."

"Just..." I say with a shrug. "You spoil me." I knew Griffin wanted some machine for his gym, so I got him that. He's hard to buy for in general, and that piece of equipment was pricey, but I saved up half the year and surprised him with it. I thought I would be the one to overspend on Christmas, but oh, no, Griffin went all out. Sometimes I still think I don't deserve him, but I promise to love him through everything forever and ever and he says that's more than enough. It's all he wants. I can give him that. I can love this man until the day I die. I think even if he left me, I'd still have done that. He's my soulmate. I didn't believe in them or true love until I met him. But he made me believe and he says I made him believe in it, too.

"I gave you what you deserved. But...there is one more thing."

"Griffin!" I scold. "You can't give me anything else. You already gave me too much. I'm going to spend the rest of the year trying to find ways to make up for it."

"How about this," he says. "How about instead, you spend the rest of the year being my fiancée?"

My heart stops and the room seems to go quiet. "What did you say?" I ask him, not believing my ears.

I meet his steely gaze, twinkling with a hint of mischief, as he repeats, clearly and confidently, "How about you spend the rest of the year being my fiancé?"

I turn fully toward him, realizing at the last second that everybody around the table really had gone quiet. They were all listening in. I don't have to look to know that they're all watching us. If I know my mom and my aunt and Griffin's parents, they're not even trying to hide it. They're just openly staring.

I'm staring, too, but at the ring box in Griffin's hand. My heart races knowing what he's asking and not believing it.

I look up into his eyes. "Are you serious?"

"I want you to be my real wife," he says with a grin. "No pretending."

I take a second just to look at him. This man is something out of a movie. He's something out of a dream come true. Who meets a girl in a bar and then hires her to work at that bar and then falls in love in that same bar? Who proposes on Christmas Day in front of both their families?

Griffin does.

"Yes," I tell him, the word breathy and rushed. All at once, time starts up again and I throw my arms around him for a kiss.

Everyone at the table cheers and we're embraced by their happiness as I kiss him again and again. "I love you so much," I tell him in between kisses.

"I know, and I love you too," he whispers against my lips and as I smile, I can feel his smile too.

There's a round of congratulations and hugs and of course, tears. This time of happiness.

"I can't wait to tell everybody at my knitting group!" my mom says and then leans closer to Griffin's mother to put a hand on her arm. "They're going to love this story."

About the Author

Thank you so much for reading my romances. I'm just a stay at home Mom and an avid reader turned Author and I couldn't be happier.

I hope you love my books as much as I do!

More by Willow Winters
www.willowwinterswrites.com/books

Made in United States
Troutdale, OR
07/02/2024

20984352R00152